· THE ·
DEVIL'S
TRILL

·THE· DEVIL'S TRILL

Daniel Moyano

Translated by Giovanni Pontiero

SERPENT'S TAIL

BRITISH LIBRARY CATALOGUING IN PUBLICATION DATA

Moyano, Daniel
The Devil's Trill
I. Title   II. El Trino del Diablo. *English*
863[F]   PQ7797. M735
ISBN 1-85242-122-3

First published as *El trino del diablo* by
Editorial Sudamericana, Buenos Aires
Copyright © 1974 by Daniel Moyano

Translation copyright © 1988 by Giovanni Pontiero

Typeset by Theatretexts

This edition first published 1988 by
Serpent's Tail, Unit 4, Blackstock Mews, London N4

Printed in Great Britain by
WBC (Print) Bristol Ltd.

Contents

1

The art of founding cities

The founding of the lost city of Todos los Santos de La Nueva Rioja was due to an error on the part of a group of Spanish army officers who misunderstood an order received from Captain-General Don Juan Ramirez de Velasco in 1591.

Upon discovering that his order had been misinterpreted, the founder enquired:

"What have you done, for God's sake?"

"There was a mistake on the map and the city was badly founded, that is to say, in the wrong place."

When he realized that to found a city in the middle of the desert, remote from other centres, in a place which was neither north, nor centre, nor north-west, could create practical difficulties in the future as well as metaphysical problems of entity, origin, and all the rest, Ramirez de Velasco thought it would be wise to cancel the deed. But the notary with the expedition, a poet from Extremadura who liked to argue, insisted that it was impossible to unfound a city or nullify the decrees drawn up in the king's name.

Ramirez and his aides met to discuss the matter and find some solution. Ramirez's adviser began to speak of futurology, and predicted great plagues, droughts, epidemics and other less serious evils for the newly founded city. The city's location in the middle of the desert would make it both hard to reach and hard to leave. The people would find no work there, food would be scarce and the more ferocious among them would take up arms against the central government. The unruly city would fall prey to military interventions, heat and flies.

When the other staff officers said they agreed with the predictions of the futurologist, Ramirez put his hands to his head.

"A fine mess," he said, adding under his breath, "you bastards."

After many hours of discussion, Ramirez and his aides decided that the problem could not be resolved by a decree. Besides, they could see certain advantages. Such a city would produce great theologians, artists of every kind and people of the future. No one can live by bread alone because, to quote the croaking scribe, we also possess an immortal soul for which we shall have to account to the Supreme Maker.

Fired with zeal, the officers considered and debated the possibilities of the new city, despite its precarious location. Ramirez, initially in favour of fresh initiatives, decided to remain silent and to listen to his aides as they thanked Providence for this error, which shortly before they had roundly condemned. The clergyman in the group, a cleanshaven fellow, defended as best he could the poor of the future, thus establishing an early precedent for today's dissident priests in the Third World. A somewhat hardline military man, seeing that Ramirez allowed everyone to speak his mind, defended the theological asceticism of the barren territory on which they had just founded the city and declared that the fertile lands, rivers and lakes should be reserved for the imperialists of the future while La Rioja, with its poverty, should be the land of eternal hope.

Ramirez de Velasco made no reply as he traced out mysterious signs with the toe of his boot. He also ordered his lieutenant to remain silent and instructed the scribe to add the following words to the act of foundation: "Moreover I declare that every person born here will receive due compensation from the King."

The founder's wise words justified the dream shared by the lieutenants who, in their enthusiasm, imagined a blissful city of men living off royal handouts. Ramirez's words, alas, evaporated into thin air because the King was to lose his colonies. They disintegrated and were consigned to the dustbins of History. The King himself fell, the centuries passed, every promise was forgotten and every transgression pardoned.

From its founding until its recent disappearance, the city was governed by chance, which, in the end, proved to be preferable to the tyranny of plans. In addition to the idiosyncracy of its geography, there was the peculiarity of its history and of its people. This is the city where the saintly San Francisco Solano arrived from Andalusia to convert the Indians by playing his violin every time they decided to rebel against the Spanish authorities. This is also the city where Triclinio was born and grew up, obscure and unknown.

"Poor Rioja," Ramirez de Velasco exclaimed when the scribe had drawn up the amendment.

"Listen," proclaimed the futurologist, "it could scarcely be more unfortunate than the nation to which it belongs."

2

Triclinio, his parents who were honey-sellers and their strategies for survival

For many years, Triclinio's parents lived off a cow, but it died on them during the civil wars, so they bought a goat instead. They fed most of their children on the goat's milk until the poor creature finally died of old age. Then Triclinio's father reflected deeply, looked at the surrounding desert and decided that a strategy for survival was called for.

He was a man fully prepared to accept substantial modifications in his own lifestyle. One day he noticed two insects go flying past. They were searching for a place where they might begin their spring mating. Since there was nothing left in the desert that could be used to build a home, the insects had lost their bearings. The old man improvised a wooden box and there he installed his first hive. By the following year, he was despatching honey to Buenos Aires, and from there to London and Rotterdam. In exchange for the honey, the old man received by way of payment large quantities of magazines, with pretty illustrations and brightly-coloured covers. Thus he acquired a vast culture which permitted him to travel in his imagination through the most desirable countries in the world. He also learned some history and succeeded in improving his beehives.

But the bees had to travel ever further to find the right flowers for producing honey and once they had exhausted the flowers of Catamarca, San Juan and other neighbouring provinces, they became as thin as Triclinio who had been fed on honey. What shall we eat if the bees should die? This child is still unable to do anything and grows thinner every day, the old man thought to himself as he observed the bees wasting away.

Triclinio's older brothers knew how to milk, how to braid leather thongs, how to geld bulls, how to ride and other such skills. They had learned all these things under a government scheme. They were registered in the local census as being skilled in these special tasks in anticipation of cattle-raising being developed in the province. The old man preferred them to be trained as cattlemen because, while earnings might be less than those paid in industry, he felt certain that the latter would be a long time coming. Besides, there was no problem about learning how to milk. They could practise once a week on the governor's cow.

His older sons, therefore, had their future assured, in the event of there being any future. But what was to become of Triclinio who was growing thinner every day?

Among the magazines which arrived from Buenos Aires there was one which caught the old man's attention. It had a feature on the life of Paganini, a musician, who, after inventing the violin, filled it with gold coins and shared the bed of Napoleon's sister. Not half bad. Triclinio was just as skinny as the diabolical violinist in the illustrations and even looked like him. Besides, if playing the violin was as difficult as the magazine claimed, then anyone who succeeded in mastering the technique would surely be well rewarded.

This secret desire absorbed the old man's thoughts for some considerable time, as he tried to find a way of making it possible for Triclinio to study something before the bees, which were becoming ever more translucent, should finally turn into air and vanish forever.

During the hot summer nights while the entire family waited outside near the olive tree for a breeze to blow, the old man tried to anchor the thoughts floating in his mind by asking his youngest son to raise one hand against the moon with outstretched fingers. And he rejoiced upon seeing there a cluster of sounds as mellifluent as those that issued from the harp of Gustavo Adolfo Becquer.

One evening as the old man sat at the river's edge, he summoned Triclinio and recounted the life of Paganini. Absorbed in his story, the old man failed to notice that the moon had disappeared and that, instead of listening, Triclinio was eagerly watching the water of the river flow past. The technique which Paganini had mastered made him the most talented violinist in all Europe. The Queen of England knelt at his feet while Napoleon's sister followed him pleading for his favours. He earned all the money in the world and then threw it into the Seine. What more could one ask of life?

The old man paused and looked at Triclinio. "Do you like that? What do you make of it?"

"Huh? Make of what?" Triclinio asked. And then: "Forgive me, I couldn't really hear you. I was listening to the water of the river and wasn't paying attention to what you were saying."

Once again, the old man was troubled by his son's constant distraction. "What's happening? Why do you never understand anything?" he tried to question him. "Because I never understand anything," was the reply. "And what happens when you don't understand anything, tell me that?" Triclinio gazed at him foolishly and asked: "What?" And the old man: "What happens when you don't understand anything?" — "My head becomes filled with sounds, that's what happens; I have all the sounds of the river in my head now and they will stay there for several days."

This was the only way in which Triclinio could make sense of the bewildering world around him.

3

About the remarkable Spumarola

About this time there arrived at La Rioja a certain
Spumarola, sent from Buenos Aires to reorganize the
Radical Party in the province. He took up residence in
the party headquarters known as the Radical House,
whose archives, because of the lack of any political
activity and the absence of elections, provided a rich
source of nutrition for the flora and fauna of the region.

Spumarola's task was to prepare the people in the
event of elections being held. Devoted to the violin, he
would spend his afternoons cooped up in the archives
where he practised various passages by Sarasate, from
which one could tell that he had had some tuition.
Fascinated by his violin — an authentic Steiner — many
people came to listen and ended up by joining the Radical
Party. So Spumarola's instrument was more effective
then his political harangues, which were not much
listened to because of his penchant for abstract words
such as peace, justice, democracy, sovereignty,
independence, liberty, individual guarantees, the rights
of man, habeas corpus etc. Good-natured like every
impoverished Italian, he could sight-read a score by
Albinoni as readily as he could understand the multitude
of plans to institutionalize politics in the country. Seeing
that there were few party members and that elections
seemed unlikely, Spumarola dedicated himself to

teaching the violin, thus converting the Radical House into a Conservatoire.

The majority of the inhabitants of La Rioja who had nothing to do apart from waiting to see what the future might bring, enrolled in the Conservatoire and in time they formed the esteemed Violin Academy of La Rioja. Since there was no orchestra in the province to play in, many musical graduates had to leave.

On the other hand, the national government later found it necessary to ban the teaching of the violin in that ancient province. This followed a suggestion by General Schönpferd, who argued in an article that all these violinists had the discipline of an army and should they ever abandon music in order to follow the path of subversion, the country would not have sufficient military resources to contain them. The article was illustrated with a photograph showing some ten thousand violinists marching on Buenos Aires, gripping their violin cases like machine guns. The caption, which was somewhat insidious given the peaceful intentions of the musicians of La Rioja, read, "Violinists or guerrillas?"

When Spumarola discovered Triclinio and saw his head filled with sounds, he was sure that he could make him into a first-class violinist and he succeeded in persuading Triclinio of this. Once he had mastered the difficult technique of playing the instrument, all his financial problems would disappear. Paganini had earned all the money he wanted and nearer home one could cite the examples of violinists like Alberto Lisy, Jaime Laredo and Ruben Gonzalez, not to mention Anahi Carfi: they were all millionaires.

In the space of a few years, Spumarola had taken Triclinio through four centuries of violin-playing which had been made progressively more complicated by violinists who had undergone psychoanalysis. Spumarola, who lacked any coherent ideas about music, believed everything that musicologists and effusive critics had written about the violin and its evolution. Triclinio, too, was encouraged to believe everything in the conviction that he was helping to create a future for the province: that future which he had heard discussed since childhood and which had turned to ashes without ever being realized.

Triclinio, withered as the surrounding landscape, became a familiar sight, wandering absent-mindedly in the streets of La Rioja, with his violin and the bees which often followed him from home all the way to the Conservatoire as in a story by Garcia Marquez. Summoned to appear before successive military governors who arrived in the city, he would put in a timid appearance at the headquarters of these temporary rulers of the province who served him coffee and made him play over and over to reassure themselves that the rumours they had heard were true. Triclinio was now famous in his native city, and had become one of the local attractions for tourists from Buenos Aires on guided tours of the province during the Folk Festival held each winter.

These were relatively happy years. Cultural life was given a boost with the promotion of flower-shows and serenades. The more important government officials, military or otherwise, offered musical tributes to the more affluent and influential residents of the province by hiring Triclinio who received a welcome, albeit modest, fee. Moreover, he benefited indirectly from the flower-shows which allowed his father to provide better nourishment for the bees, resulting in larger consignments of old magazines from Buenos Aires.

But the custom of having flower-shows and serenades passed, and investigative commissions came into fashion. Influenced by Schönpferd's article, one of these commissions asserted that Spumarola and his violinists were inciting violence throughout the province and that this could prejudice the long-awaited future. After investigating the Spumarola affair, the government issued a decree denouncing him as a conspirator, an intellectual, and *persona non grata*.

At the moment of parting, Triclinio tried to express his sorrow, but Spumarola told him not to worry for he was on his way. Be wary of women, wine and folk music. A woman can disturb the reflexes which are so essential for playing an instrument. You will have time for such distractions when you make your first tour of Europe. What you need right now is a good violin, which isn't easy to find. Another thing: nothing is ever likely to change here. You must go to Buenos Aires like everyone else. A local priest has expressed interest in your future on a number of occasions. You must go and see him and ask for his advice. Remember to get some relaxation and watch what you eat. A little gentle exercise, regular walks and a good swim every now and then.

The old teacher, who was also regarded as an apostate by the Radical Party, mounted the faithful mule which had brought him and began the return journey to Buenos Aires, a little poorer than before, much older and terrifyingly close to the horrors of retirement.

4

How sounds saved Triclinio

Throughout the years of Triclinio's training, the city, as predicted by the Spanish futurologists, became increasingly impoverished. When the predicted plagues arrived, walls were built around the city; and when it was realized that these were useless because the plagues were spreading underground, trenches were dug which were equally useless although they helped to prevent the blackmarket trade with the coast. The drawbridge erected to prevent the inhabitants from escaping served no purpose. Those who could not escape physically left by metaphysical means or some equally mysterious route, like the pupils of Spumarola who disappeared from the region with their instruments and who are still being pursued for fear that the presence of these starving violinists scattered throughout the provinces might provoke a chain reaction.

Once they saw the futility of defence mechanisms in trying to protect themselves from calamity, the people had recourse to charms brought from a factory in Avellaneda, but even the charms contracted endemic diseases. Later they were used by the lumpen proletariat as offerings to the saints in order to ward off unemployment.

Submarines capable of cutting a passage through land arrived from the Pacific right underneath the province and soaked dry its subterranean waters, while the old women and the children walked in procession with their Patron Saint and prayed for rain.

This state of affairs provoked another intervention by the federal government, a fresh investigation and massive vaccinations against everything. Meanwhile, Triclinio, impervious to what was happening because of the sounds that filled his head, mastered 195 new strokes with his violin bow.

As a result of this fresh enquiry, the national government ordered a Solar Observatory to be built in the city, thereby promoting a local passion for astronomy. The ancient cult of worshipping virgins carved from wooden poles was replaced by the cult of Urania. The entire population observed the sky attentively, eager to understand the first principles of this science and to understand the names which men throughout the ages had given to the stars. Triclinio's parents managed to arrange that, in exchange for their honey, they would get astronomy books from Buenos Aires instead of Batman comics.

The books were circulated widely and the people acquired a great deal of knowledge about cosmology in the hope of finding employment in the new Observatory. But the only person to be hired was a photographer who took daily pictures of the sun and developed the plates which were then sent to Germany.

Things being so, an official of the Military Government who held a revisionist view of history decided to rehabilitate the Montonero guerrillas, and some days later the provincial capital was peacefully invaded by 12,000 veterans on horseback who had travelled from the interior with lances and pikes. The old men believed they saw in the government's stance an opportunity to improve their image, but, given that they were still alive, this was not yet on the cards; as guerrilla fighters they were real, just as the government was real and history was real. The situation remained hopeless and nothing was likely to change. They were forced to sign a non-aggression pact and in return they were promised water if it should rain, a pact so blatantly dishonest that, although the veterans could no longer hear or see because they were living in the past, the horses that had brought them turned angrily towards the desert as they dragged away the corpses-to-be of their old masters.

Finally, the children were taken to other provinces to ensure their survival as well as that of the shoe-shiners' trade union. Only the old people stayed behind, surviving on their memories. Triclinio's parents began to die with the last of the bees, but instead of bemoaning as before that Triclinio did not possess a more reliable strategy for survival, they were glad that he was content with his violin, remote from words, from a reality which had become meaningless, from decrees, his head full of pleasant sounds which warded off fear.

The city itself, like its inhabitants, adopted survival strategies. The trains were banned – trains which normally carried the region's meagre products to Buenos Aires and brought back papers, especially newspapers and magazines with pictures of naked women — which led to an alarming increase in the birth rate. News bulletins from the province were also banned and the entire city was covered with a huge circus tent with the mountains of Velasco and Famatina as supports. Anyone who wanted to know what was happening in the province had to pay an entrance fee in addition to a modest tax which was received by Buenos Aires as payment for the privilege of being integrated into the national territory.

Things were no better in Buenos Aires, where they reintroduced the instruments of torture burned in 1813. In order to save the nation, the government issued austerity measures, prohibiting destitution, hunger, endemic illnesses, infant mortality, the high cost of living, protests, and the desire for procreation.

When Triclinio's parents saw that it was becoming increasingly difficult to survive, that the country was full of moths and cockroaches and that the recent tax on bee-keeping had finished off even the bees, they decided that the hour had come to die.

So they sent for Triclinio and, after begging him to neither weep nor mourn, they informed him of their decision to die rather than witness even greater evils.

Triclinio remained pensive for a moment, without betraying any emotion, for he already knew of their decision and received their news in silence. His parents' resolve to die was predictable, it had been in the air for some considerable time.

The old man stretched out on his pallet and the old woman knelt down beside him. Triclinio, standing motionless in the middle of the room, felt the place gradually become empty. This was the one moment when there were no sounds in his head, so the old man seized the opportunity of saying more or less the following words: "I don't know where you can possibly go with your violin now, but may God bless you, my son. Just one thing: I read in one of those dreadful magazines from Buenos Aires that Paganini would have come to nothing if it had not been for his Stradivarius and Guarnerius, expensive instruments possessed only by nobles and altruists. We have always been poor in this immensely rich country, so we have nothing to leave you, especially not a decent violin. But I have heard that a priest in our neighbourhood has a collection of excellent violins from various countries. Try to see him and persuade him to give you one. I think he gave a violin to that lanky Brizuelita who emigrated during the crisis and went on to play with all the major symphony orchestras throughout the world. And another thing: unless you are forced to, never abandon our native province. One day things may change. Who knows. That's all, my son. I wish I was not leaving you in this world with something as complicated as the violin. It's all we have to give you. Try to use it for everyone's benefit. Be good, if that still means anything. And try not to lose hope. If you trust in providence, that will give you the strength to carry on in the long run and convince you that you can still trust in something. And now would you play for me?"

Triclinio tuned up and, using harmonics and *flautati*, he succeeded in imitating the rustic flute so loved by his father.

Raising one hand as if to wave goodbye, the old man told him that was how Chopin had died, listening to music. "I read that in one of the magazines."

5

The story of a man who lived in a city where he was not needed

Having failed in his attempts to join the city orchestra which played folk music and did not require any violinists, Triclinio visited the families who, in the past, had hired him to give serenades. They informed him that serenades had been denounced as immoral by the government and had consequently been banned. Others told him that the Military Governor would have overlooked the measure of eroticism there might be in a serenade, but had decided to prohibit them once and for all when several prisoners, including a bishop, escaped from the prison where they were awaiting the verdict of an anti-subversive investigation as they were listening to a serenade which, according to information supplied by the CIA, was a coded signal.

Triclinio then approached courting couples. He promised that his violin music would help them to experience the joys of love with even greater intensity. But the couples replied that they had decided to go on a love strike as a protest against torture, and that there would be no more courting couples until they were certain that love was not simply one more snare to curtail freedom and land them in prison. We want love to be made available to all, irrespective of age, and the abolition of censorship. And we shall go on with the strike until our happiness is restored.

He stopped at a street corner and played in the hope that someone might like his music and offer him something. Many stopped to listen and gave him IOUs or vouchers which could be exchanged for money in the event of the donors finding work.

At the restaurant they accepted the IOUs and he was able to eat an ostrich stew. When he tried to resume playing that same afternoon, the local authorities intervened because the music had upset the 50,000 dogs that roamed the city and its outskirts. The dogs looked up and howled, transfixed by sounds they had never heard before.

Later he was arrested and taken to the police station. Unable to produce his musician's licence or to pay the corresponding fine, he was forced to look on in dismay while they stained his violin with ink in order to take fingerprints.

Once the police had confirmed that Triclinio's violin had no connection with the violins referred to by Schönpferd, he was released one dank morning, after they had searched his house from top to bottom and rummaged through his old shoes and the pages of his diary, which he had to explain since it was written in musical notation.

"They are musical themes which I jot down," Triclinio told them dispiritedly, "for my head is always filled with sounds. During the whole time that I was imprisoned, I couldn't hear anything except the rhythm of *Eine Kleine Nachtmusik* which is the rhythm of my freedom. I didn't feel the time passing or that I was in prison, for in reality I was elsewhere, tra la la la, eating honey for breakfast with my parents and reading magazines by the river's edge, tra la la la la la."

When Triclinio returned home, he found that everything had been ransacked by the police, his pictures were beneath the mattresses on the floor, the beds were resting up against the walls, the pages of music had been fed into a computer and the music-stands overturned. All his memories, such as they were, had been exposed and developed. Upon realizing that even his thoughts had been disinfected, he leaned on a broken music-stand and shed a momentary tear, swearing that he would never more weep or return to this house which, at this point, was taken over by the police who needed more space in which to put their prisoners.

Then he burned the empty beehives, grabbed his violin, walked out of the house, and bade farewell to the past which was all he possessed. The violin tucked under his arm felt light, the ground beneath his feet was soft, the future opened before him; it was a lovely day and Triclinio neither expected nor longed for anything.

He was about to abandon his native province, but he decided to make a fresh effort to comply with his father's wishes. The director of the Institute of Culture, to whom Triclinio turned for help, a man practised in all the arts, read him the decrees safeguarding the Argentine nation's cultural heritage. The director explained that it was impossible to find him a job in the department of music, unless he played the drum or the guitar. The decree specified that La Rioja was to concentrate on folk music, thus reserving for cosmopolitan Buenos Aires all other types of music. "I think you'll have to emigrate. All those who studied music with Spumarola have paid for the experience with exile. But perhaps you should try your luck with the President of the Department of History and Literature. I believe he needs a violinist."

The President had been an outstanding horseman on the Cordillera before he took up historical research. He had close family ties with the army as well as being a personal friend of the President of the Republic.

In fact, he did need a violinist, but not a professional musician. "I know you play well and are familiar with the classical repertoire, but all I want is someone who can impersonate San Francisco Solano for the historical tableau in the main square, to be followed by a procession. I want someone who is prepared to wear the Franciscan habit and simply hold a violin in his hands. Obviously if it were someone who could play, and play well, it would be much more interesting. The problem is that we don't know what kind of music the saint played. That's the information we need before we can ask for any modification of the decree governing the national division and geographical distribution of music. If we had evidence that the saint played classical music, then we could prove that the traditions of this region are not based on folk music but on something much more serious. We could then question the criteria of the military which restrict us to folk music. We might even form a small orchestra and then you could stay here. But if it is proved that the saint played folk music, even Spanish music, then you either pack your bags or take up the guitar."

The President of the Academy, however, was unable to prove anything for want of sufficient evidence. So when he was asked to submit a report on Triclinio's situation to the authorities, he declared that it was yet another case of deviation from national and provincial norms. According to his report, an official of the Radical Party who was an amateur violinist had arrived in the province many years ago and had taught the intricacies of violin technique to a group of young men who were converted to subversion by the experience. With the departure of Spumarola, the root cause of the trouble disappeared, but Triclinio was left behind, the last victim of these misguided politics.

Then the police altered Triclinio's civil status. Instead of being a "compulsory resident", he became a "displaced person", in other words, one step away from exile.

6

Triclinio travels in melody

"This city doesn't exist. Have you noticed that? Now you have no choice but to go to Buenos Aires and leave us without a violinist. Have you been listening to me?" the priest continued.

Triclinio still had the rhythm of *Eine Kleine Nachtmusik* in his head, and so the priest's words for him were nothing but a few monosyllables in the middle of a pause, which didn't interfere with the music's Mozartian structure. The priest was familiar with this peculiarity in Triclinio, for he, too, sometimes had a little tune in his head. But unlike Triclinio, he had failed to discover that this could be a way of being happy.

When the youth told him about the proposition made by the President of the Academy of History and Literature, the priest dismissed it with a scornful gesture and assured him that San Francisco Solano only played folk music. "And he played very badly. I don't believe he converted any Indians with his music, unless they happened to be hard of hearing. But tell me. Who put the idea of playing the violin into your head? Violins are luxury instruments and have been prized as such for hundreds of years. I have seen in Florence violins that were veritable jewels of sensibility and craftsmanship. But no one wants violinists here. Where will you go with your violin? Not that you can call that thing a violin.

No, no, don't take it out, I don't want to see it. It can't be up to much. There's no way you could afford a good violin. Or a beautiful woman. You need money for such luxuries, and here there is no money or anything that resembles it. Who taught you the violin? Spumarola, no doubt. Have you ever seen a real violin? Although, when all is said and done, I suppose the only sensible thing to do in this city is to play the violin."

He said all this as he passed, followed by Triclinio, from one room to another as if searching for something. He paused before a large cupboard which contained some fifty violins. Triclinio gazed at them, but when he tried to reach out to touch one of them, the priest intervened, warning him to be careful because the instrument was a Maggini, and while he might be prepared to give it to him, Triclinio was not to touch it just yet.

"From now onwards, you must strive for perfection if you want to become one of the chosen few who have conquered the world with the violin. I bet you don't know your harmonics. An old maestro once said that if a good violinist is like a prince, then the harmonics are the diamonds in his crown. Also remember the *flautato* and the *pizzicato*, with the fingers of the left hand. Once you've mastered all these, even audiences in Buenos Aires will sit up and listen. I'm going to send you to a monastery, where you can stay until you've learned your harmonics. When you've mastered them, everyone will respect you. I'll also give you a list of influential people to contact."

"The Bishop?" counterpointed Triclinio.

"I don't think he's our man. With your name and face, and coming as you do from an impoverished province, he'll think you're from the Third World and make you play the violin for their prisoners. Have nothing to do with people from the Third World or with those who complain and protest. Go on studying the violin, that is the best you can hope for in this world. Once you start complaining and protesting, they will come knocking at your door, and then the only solution is to grab your suitcase and move on.

The suspense of his imminent departure prevented Triclinio from sampling the meat pies they were serving in the sacristy. The bus was leaving for Buenos Aires at two o'clock in the afternoon and there was little time left. The priest opened another cupboard and, pointing to ten more violins inside, told him to take the one right at the back. Triclinio opened the case and removed the violin from its silk cover. First he tested it with a simple *pizzicato*, then with a stroke of his bow. A miraculous sound, they both agreed. "This is the violin that San Francisco Solano played," the priest told him. "The Indians must have been converted the moment they saw it. Isn't it marvellous? You will have to change the fingerboard. The wood is slightly pitted there in the first position, in the manner of a tango violin. Which confirms what I told you about the saint. In Buenos Aires they will charge you a fortune to repair it. But you must take it to the Frenchman even though he will up the cost when he knows where it comes from, since he can always spot a rare instrument and he's sure to find out. Obviously, I shall have to pay for it since I've never met anyone as hard up as you."

The priest picked up the Maggini and they tuned their instruments. Then they rummaged through an impressive collection of scores, laughing and amused for no apparent reason. They set up scores for the violin duets by Viotti on the music-stand, haunting melodies which can transport the listener into "a timeless world of sounds, where musicians rejoiced in other mansions, where every gesture and tremor of the soul echoed through the air", to quote a former owner of the scores who remains anonymous but was clearly addicted to fine words and high-sounding phrases.

After they finished playing, Triclinio examined the violin at some length. "Everyone thinks it's lost and no one knows that it has been here," the priest said. "I am confident that it will be safe with you. Cherish it all your life. And whenever you take it out of its case to study or play, leave it for twenty to thirty minutes so that the instrument becomes acclimatized to the room temperature. Buenos Aires has an abominable climate. From time to time, leave it out in the sun for a short period. Don't let the rosin accumulate near the bridge. Be careful with the bow, which is French. And above all, don't tell anyone that the violin belonged to the saint, otherwise they will take it from you and display it in some museum of religious art."

At the bus station the priest, still giving advice, shed baptismal tears. "Keep away from women, and young curates from the monasteries, and don't listen to what they tell you. Be sure to practise your scales."

Just before he boarded the bus, the police demanded to see Triclinio's certificate of exile before they would allow him to leave. Then the priest showed them the card which classified Triclinio as "a displaced person", and convinced them that there was no real theological difference between the terms *displaced* and *exiled*. The police were persuaded.

Throughout the journey, the memory of the music for second violin which the priest had played in the Viotti duet prevented Triclinio from taking in the barren landscape of his native province and, later on, the humid pampas. Buenos Aires suddenly loomed into sight as if simply divided from La Rioja by the melody which had been going through his head for more than a thousand kilometres.

7

On the invisible heart of the fair homeland

One month after his arrival, Triclinio was still bewildered by this capital which shone with so much wealth. He walked its streets rhythmically with a tra la la, staring at the festive shop windows and the beautiful women, with a tra la la la la. This was a blissful city, and from now on nothing associated with La Rioja existed. The serenades were gone; so were the Institute of Culture, and the barefooted urchins, and the political harangues, and the outbreaks of famine, and the priest with the violins, and the plan for rural health, and the social welfare for mothers and their offspring, and the distribution of powdered milk to those children who survived to the age of two, and the project to clear the slums, and the annual week of festivities in La Rioja, and the campaign against the high cost of living, and the Centre for Folklore. Nothing, nothing of all this seemed ever to have existed, not the peaceful campaign of anti-nuclear defence, nor Chagas fever, nor the campaign against goitre and immorality, nor alcoholism, nor the traditional hospitality of the inhabitants of La Rioja, nor federal co-partnership funds, nor the brothels, nor the casino, nor the bass drum, nor the federal defeat at the Battle of Pozo de Vargas, nor Facundo's reign of terror in La Rioja, nor El Chacho, nor Felipe Varela's campaign for local autonomy, nor its twenty thousand street pedlars, nor even its seven hundred clubs, nothing, nothing, all of it seemed to fade without trace in the smog which floated over the blissful city. This is my homeland. And why not? Tra la la la.

And since the priest had forgotten to give him the address of the monastery where he would find shelter, he was obliged to stay in a boarding-house near the city centre. The landlord gave him permission to practise the violin every evening between five forty-eight and one minute past eleven, provided he used a mute when he played.

He had been practising for an hour (*sostenuti*, long strokes with the bow, breath control) when a string broke. Finding himself without any spares, he went down to ask the landlord where he could find a shop that specialized in music supplies. "Try the kiosk on the corner, and why don't you buy some rosin for your bow? Yours doesn't seem to work too well in this climate. You're not from round here, are you?" the landlord asked him.

The kiosk stocked not only strings of varying quality, but also music-stands, scores, rosin, chin-rests, supports, and all the other accessories used by violinists. The kiosk on the next corner even had violins for sale. This was heaven. For several hundred metres the shopkeepers competed for trade by means of neon signs and an ever larger selection of goods, combining eroticism and music to increase their sales.

When he returned, the landlord informed Triclinio that, because he had been so long in coming back, he had given his practice period to another violinist. "I had no idea that there were any other violinists living here," said Triclinio. The landlord looked surprised: "Here everyone is a violinist, all these boarding-houses cater for violinists, so do some of the hotels. No. You're not dreaming. In Buenos Aires everyone plays the violin but not to earn a living as you seem to think. Forgive me for meddling. Here people earn their living in the meat trade and only play the violin to combat what you might call a sort of spleen we've inherited from the English. And now, if you'll excuse me, I must try to get in a little practice myself."

Triclinio was somewhat taken aback by the landlord's biting tone, but it turned out he was a decent sort of chap. He gave Triclinio tickets for concerts and cooked excellent rump steaks. And despite his haggard expression, he seemed content. One afternoon he told Triclinio: "Once I was young and a violinist like you, when life was still worth living in this country. But when I was a student, I got obsessed with a woman, and gambling on horses and inflation did the rest. Any tango could tell my story. But I'm not complaining. I have good customers and get the odd bribe whenever I report to the government any pseudo-violinists carrying arms instead of a violin inside their instrument case. You know how it is. But I have some news for you: the Civic Symphony Orchestra at the Ministry of the Interior has a vacancy for a third violinist. Why don't you try for it?"

Although the competition was won by a retired lieutenant who played the violin for the same reason as everyone else as well as on medical advice, Triclinio gave a brilliant performance in the optional pieces. Out of almost twenty thousand contestants, only he and the lieutenant reached the last round. The latter was a lieutenant *sui generis* who possessed a Germanic flair for music. And if he didn't quite match Triclinio's bravura and imagination, he showed greater precision and a deeper knowledge of music, which gave him the edge. Having heard of the remarkable sound produced by the violin of this dark-haired youth, dignitaries from the nearby regions attended the final heats of the competition, while plain-clothes policemen maintained order by training their guns discreetly on the audience.

When the players had shown their skills in Sarasate, Vieuxtemps and Paganini, the jury asked them to improvise and to state where their style of playing came from. Triclinio first improvised on the decline of the bees, then on a poem by Martinez Estrada extolling the artistry of the violinist and then, amidst the applause of the public, police and officials, declared: "That is how one plays in the invisible heart of my fair homeland." He felt so self-conscious as he uttered this clichéd phrase that he sensed it might lose him the contest. The jury, however, was delighted with Triclinio's formal gesture, for he had played on only one string.

The lieutenant stepped forward, cut the four strings of his violin and, after breaking his bow into several pieces, recited in a melodious voice the poem by Martinez Estrada, to the wild enthusiasm of his audience, and declared: "That is how one plays in the residence of the President of the Republic," which was all too true and won him the contest.

As Triclinio was putting away his instrument, an official from the Ministry came up to congratulate him and confided that the jury had wavered in its decision despite the lieutenant's skilful performance, "because your violin sounds like the music of the gods. Where on earth did you get it?" Triclinio's wry expression made him look sad, so the official took him aside and provided him with a reference which would secure him a job in a factory that pickled ox-tongues.

This new job, added to the two he had already, meant that he could afford to move to a quieter boarding-house where he could continue his violin studies.

8

The epic war of the radio stations

One evening at the far end of the little courtyard of the new boarding-house where all the city's noises reverberate: the ships' sirens, the shouts from the football pitches, the street orchestras, the explosion of tear-gas grenades, exchange rates for the dollar and solemn pronouncements; one evening in this corner of Buenos Aires whose streets had lost their innocence, Triclinio, overcome by sadness, held back a tear.

Then, recalling an image he had seen on television, he retired to his room, a room redolent of the past, and began writing a letter:

Dear President: it is me who is writing. After experiencing the most abject poverty in my native province, which even now I have sadly forgotten, I have spent years studying the violin in order to have some skill which might earn me a living and spare me the hunger endured by many of my fellow provincials who are forced to sell figs, spring onions, meat pies and home-made bread, as well as the magazines and newspapers which are printed in our illustrious capital and reach the provinces by the truck-load and keep everyone happy. La Rioja is a city teeming with street pedlars from the early hours of the morning. It is difficult to know what it is they are selling, because instead of words, they use a kind of wail and they pass so quickly that if one does happen to hear them call out their wares and go out to buy something, they have already disappeared round the next corner with their mournful wailing. Then the vegetable sellers arrive with loudspeakers and offer their produce to the housewives who gather on the street corners to see what is being sold. Then those terrifying motorcyclists arrive, zooming backwards and forwards all day long. At night it is the turn of the folk musicians whose singing is relayed from the clubs by loudspeakers. They express the latest misfortunes in our provinces, which are transformed into something wonderful in these songs because the landscape is always beautiful although the people who live there may think otherwise. And so night advances, and when the musicians fall silent, cockerels start to crow, announcing the return of the street sellers. I had hoped to create a more beautiful sound than a street seller's cry, or a political speech, or a carnival guitar or a cockerel's crow to offer to my native province but, after making enormous sacrifices in order to master the difficult technique of playing the violin, I discovered that my province did not need any violinists, so I came here where everyone plays the violin. That, Mr President, is my awkward situation. Can you grant me an interview to see whether there might be some solution to my problem? Yours affectionately, Triclinio.

The interview was arranged for two months hence "so long as affairs of state permit". Just as he was about to enter the presidential palace, Triclinio saw in the transfixed eyes of a soldier a column of tanks approaching down the Avenida de Mayo with the clear intention of overthrowing the president.

He was received in a small reception room crammed with various statues from the sanctuary of the Virgin of Lujan, to whom the president was much devoted.

"They're all from different periods," the president told him as he switched on the radio to listen to the first proclamation by the rebels. "They have seized several radio stations on which they are broadcasting their grievances," he went on to explain.

Standing at the president's side was his father confessor, a clergyman quite unlike the music-loving curate of La Rioja. "Don't resign, don't choose exile, don't commit suicide," the priest urged as the president tuned in to another station on which the rebels were denouncing him and announcing that a hundred and ninety-nine tanks were advancing from Magdalena ripping up all the highways. The president switched on several radios simultaneously in order to listen to loyal stations listing the achievements of the government which was being overthrown. When he heard one station announce that order had been restored throughout the nation, that the revolt had been suppressed and that cleaning-up operations were already under way, the president smiled and gave Triclinio a knowing wink, as if to reassure him that the revolt had undoubtedly failed and that Triclinio's career as a violinist was safe as long as the president remained in office and in control.

All of a sudden, loud explosions could be heard coming from the radio stations manned by the rebels. The priest advised Triclinio to leave. The president was about to say: "There's no danger. You are listening to a broadcast," when he saw the priest pointing at the young musician's sensitive eardrums, and the president nodded in agreement.

Then they showed him the gallery of deposed presidents. There were oil paintings here, the portraits of all the presidents who had been overthrown in the course of the past hundred and fifty years. Triclinio caught a glimpse of an artist concealed behind a pile of books who was furtively committing to canvas the physical traits of the reigning president.

A grenade landed in the president's office which made the father confessor reel and amused the president, who within the last few minutes had put on a mask which gave adequate protection not only against nerve and tear-gas, but also against nausea gas. In response to this outrageous attack, the president poked his head out of the window and shouted to the rebels that, unlike the last civilian president or those students who rampaged daily on the streets of Buenos Aires, it would take more than tear-gas to intimidate him. If they wanted to dislodge him, the rebels would have to use armed force.

When more grenades landed in his office, the president grabbed the microphone connected to one of the radio stations remaining loyal and declared a state of emergency. Meanwhile the radio stations held by the rebels rallied the nation with a persuasive message: "Say yes to change and prove that the change is yours, that you wanted it and that you made it possible. Argentina deserves a better destiny, don't let your country down."

"These degenerates," one of the president's aides observed, "have hired experts in media propaganda. We're done for."

The father confessor suggested to the president that, in order to avoid the futile sacrifice of the presidential guards who had sworn their allegiance, he should surrender during the midnight changing of the guard, but the president refused, insisting that he could not renounce his principles, that he would go down fighting and that he did not carry arms for fun.

Triclinio never discovered what happened after that for he was immediately ordered to leave. Moreover, one of the transistors of his pocket radio was broken. The president's palace was surrounded by tanks and soldiers. In the distance, at the far end of the Avenida de Mayo, the illuminated Congress looked like a castle. Triclinio suddenly felt sorry for the president. He found himself thinking about all the children back in his native province who would be deprived of their president, and have no one periodically to promise them tins of powdered milk.

When he arrived at his boarding-house, he tried to tune in to the radio stations still loyal to the government, but these had already been captured by the rebels, who were now loyal to another president. A cloying voice declared in affected tones: "Now your skin will experience the mystery of a strange caress: at last you will possess the forbidden, for the forbidden is now law."

Triclinio huddled in the corner of his tiny room and felt that he had started to grow old.

9

The theory and practice of floating

One day as he was floating along one of the streets that run southwards, Triclinio, having shown his papers to various police patrols, became aware that the only thing permitted was hope. But he could not take this thought any further because the sounds, which had momentarily stopped, began to fill his head once more.

During these truces he did not know whether to regret that he could not use his understanding in the normal way or to rejoice that the sounds enabled him to ignore the fact that he no longer had a city to return to, that he was unwelcome in that country he had heard about at school but which now seemed to belong more to history than to reality.

Sometimes he took advantage of these lulls to nourish his hopes but without success, for he was not sure exactly what those hopes were or could possibly contain. Sometimes, on the other hand, he tried to rid himself of the sounds in order to find a way of understanding. For some time now, he had wanted to know about the world and himself, without the terrifying abstraction of rhythms and notes, but on the rare occasion when he succeeded, he could not clarify his thoughts for instead of sounds, words throbbed through his head, phrases which he had heard or which had occurred to him or which were inspired by statues and monuments;

resounding words that embellished history and served no real purpose. So he recalled the sounds; somehow they seemed kinder than events.

Now that he did not know his whereabouts, he felt more at ease. He had no home, no family and no forebodings, and to play the violin was no longer an overwhelming desire but a secret gift which he could keep for better days. At times he felt nostalgia for his native province, but when he thought of the military governors, the smell of motorcycle exhausts and the cries of impoverished street sellers, his nostalgia soon vanished. And when he thought of the Llanos, of the elderly who no longer even had memories to help them survive, and of the sporadic outbreaks of famine and drought, he felt his roots vacillate. Where is my homeland? he would then ask himself, evoking memories of his school-days. In Buenos Aires he had already seen the old colonial town hall, which was a great deal smaller than the town halls he had sketched in his notebooks; the Pyramid on the Avenida de Mayo which was as small as he remembered it, and the presidential palace which he had actually visited. Everything appeared strange to him, as in a picture.

As he wandered through endless streets, oscillating between those haunting sounds and the sterile contemplation of new buildings, Triclinio realized that he was floating. It was far from easy. It required an almost imperceptible process of training which then took on all the characteristics of a technique. A bit like a fish learning to swim, the difference being that Triclinio floated. In order to float, it was not necessary to remain still and wait for the wind to carry him along: the very presence of atmosphere enabled him to float. A good floater, he thought, is not someone without a fixed target.

Quite the contrary: it meant having not one but many objectives which become combined, become invisible. A good floater was much like a trapeze artist, whose performance involves risks that are rewarded by the triumph of flight. The floater has only the risk of the trapeze artist, since flight is the preserve of angels or those who take their place.

Bewildered by all this, Triclinio arrived at the other end of the town. He looked at the deserted streets, at the dripping walls, and had a moment's fear that some police patrol might interrupt his floating. He found in his jacket the certificate of exile issued by the police back in his native province, and felt more relaxed.

Turning a corner, he heard a choir of girls and saw that they were dressed in fine white linen. This vision took him back to his recent childhood, and guided by the girls' heavenly singing and by the beauty of their legs, he followed them for some considerable way, all the way to the gates of a large factory where they worked making the thread that ties sausages. He also saw that several groups of soldiers and policemen, with tanks and the oddest vehicles equipped with tear-gas, dogs, giraffes and bedbugs, were getting ready to prevent the girls from entering the factory. They were under orders from military headquarters, who had been informed by the intelligence services that the girls intended to occupy the factory as a protest against their low wages.

It took just one large cloud of gas emitted from one of the vehicles to make the girls vanish into thin air. The dogs, watching with one eye while they went on being dogs with the other, sniffed Triclinio, and when they failed to detect any smell because of his status as a displaced person, they allowed him to enter the area, which was under military control. This automatically

triggered the hydraulic mechanism of the vehicles, and
Triclinio found himself being sprayed with liquids of
varying colour, density and pressure. He fled as best he
could, while the sound of the National Anthem filled his
head, mingled with the strains of a lullaby and the tune
the girls were singing before they vanished. He felt as if
he could barely walk, as if his legs were spiked with
thorns. Crossing a street, he spotted some houses and,
clutching his identity card, he fell to his knees.

10

America

A group of shabbily dressed, unshaven, menopausal men came up to Triclinio to give him a hand. "I didn't know this place existed," Triclinio confided, upon recovering his speech, as he looked at the incredible squalor of the surrounding houses. Despite the overall poverty, the houses were nicely decorated; the entire district was really nothing but façade. There were two little streets in the shape of the letter S on each side of an elevated bridge, above which they hoisted by way of a flag a large music key made from barbed wire taken from the barricades. They told him that this was Violinville, an emergency shantytown where violinists without a future were living.

The district was set out in the shape of a violin, separated from the city by small lagoons, a swamp and a railway track, whose curve bounded the right-hand side of the instrument. It comprised a number of sectors, each of them corresponding to a specific part of the violin. Some of the musicians lived on the fingerboard, the more affluent members of the community were settled on the bridge, and others on the chin-rest, while those who lived on the pegs were unmistakably the poorest.

They took him to live in a hut made of sheet-metal situated near the D-peg which overlooked a more congenial neighbourhood. Here there was some daily human contact, for it was inhabited by social workers who had come to make a study of the slums and, in order to familiarize themselves with the place, had decided to build their own shantytown.

"These are people who take an interest in our problems, as if they had been sent by the government, which they are not. They are nice people, but don't know the first thing about music," the group explained to him.

They found him a corner in a room occupied by six violinists who, like all the other inhabitants of the shantytown, had deformed hands and arthritis in their fingers from lack of exercise; for no one possessed an instrument in Violinville.

The houses had become pink because every time disturbances broke out in the city centre, the water-cannons passed and the police sprayed the demonstrators with coloured water. Time and time again, the inhabitants had pleaded with the authorities not to spray water. They pointed out that they were not responsible for the disturbances and that the water was discolouring the walls of their homes and making their rheumatism and arthritis worse. In the end they gave up, for every time they complained they received yet another visit from a commission of enquiry. Their homes were turned upside down and the fragile fabric of their huts was disturbed. Floors were dug up and mattresses overturned. All the inhabitants had had their fingers stained two or three times and suffered great pain as their fingers, deformed by arthritis, were stretched to make contact with the wooden blocks used for fingerprinting.

Triclinio slept badly that night because of the pains in his legs, and every time the wind blew, the numerous metal objects hanging on the walls started shaking and clanking. There were also various musical instruments made by fashioning tinplate into forms, which produced sounds when the wind became strong. There were also knick-knacks made from old tins, musical scores composed with tacks, washers, bolts and other unidentified objects.

After sharing a plump herring caught by one of the six violinists, they sang the *Ave Verum* before settling down to sleep. When he awoke next morning, Triclinio told the others that he could not get up because the pain in his legs was so bad. No sooner had he spoken than a middle-aged social worker came into the room and started to examine his legs.

"I don't like the look of this," he said. "Morphological examination reveals that you have received at least five blasts from the water cannons."

He took a pair of eyebrow tweezers and set about trying to remove several plastic bullets which were embedded in Triclinio's skin and were almost invisible. The social worker explained that these bullets had penetrated his skin when he was squirted with water. Nearly all the bullets had already been absorbed into his blood and it was this that was causing the pain.

"Unfortunately," he added, "they are insensitive to Röntgen rays and it is impossible to detect them on an X-ray; besides, since they disintegrate on making contact with surgical instruments, we cannot make the normal tests. We should, however, tell Ufa when she arrives. She might be able to use her influence and persuade the police to stop these atrocities. Don't worry, friend. Within the next three days, you'll be as right as rain."

Using crutches loaned by the social worker, Triclinio spent his three days of convalescence travelling from the neighbourhood near the pegs all the way down to the tailpiece. Certain districts were inhabited by retired violinists who did not suffer from arthritis and who, while waiting for their pension to come through, spent their days arguing the merits of the ancient music school of Danclas. They were, however, stricken with arterio-sclerosis, a disease which inclined them to offer eloquent but useless words of wisdom about life and other matters. He made the acquaintance of the shantytown's oldest inhabitant and founder. He did not suffer from arthritis, and was the only one there who studied the violin for eight hours every day despite being without an instrument. As Triclinio entered, the old man, who was practising, interrupted his exercises to greet him.

"One day," he assured Triclinio, after hearing about his situation, "we shall be free to play again and then we must resume our place in society. Meanwhile we mustn't despair or lose heart but carry on playing every day as if everything were fine."

Having spoken these words, the great maestro continued to practise his scales in thirds on an imaginary violin which, by obliging him to adopt the correct posture, helped him to maintain his athletic figure. He had been a soloist at the world-famous Teatro Colon before falling into disgrace because of some scheming minister who had him summoned before a counter-subversion tribunal. He was acquitted only because his judges knew nothing about the theory of the scale in fifths.

He also made the acquaintance of a famous violinist who had been crippled by a tear-gas grenade which had shattered his kneecap as he was leaving the Colon. He too had no violin, but having been reared among the orange groves of Tucuman at a time when Tucuman still produced oranges, he knew how to draw sounds from the leaf of an orange tree. Folded with care, the leaf could be used to produce a sound which closely resembled the violin. And although he had been expelled from the inner city for trying to form a trade union for crippled violinists, he had disguised himself as a tramp (which in fact he was), and every afternoon he stopped on a corner of Corrientes to play his leaf, collecting the money which the foreign tourists gave him in order one day to buy a real violin. He had been saving up for fifteen years, eating just enough to survive, and he had collected enough money to buy the violin many times over. But every time he contemplated a purchase, the price of violins soared due to inflation, the nation's dwindling assets and the Ministry of Economic Affairs. He had to hop along on one leg when he wanted to get about, but he stayed cheerful and did not lose his sense of humour and capacity for work. Close to his hut grew an orange tree which as yet yielded no fruit despite the city's climate, but did manage to sprout the leaves necessary to produce the ever more harmonious sounds.

In general, Triclinio saw that these people formed a community both happy and sad, where there were neither fears nor expectations. And although at first sight it gave the impression of being a prison without guards, he felt safe there for the first time since leaving his native province. It was as if he had found a true homeland.

It was almost night when he returned to the hut he shared with the six violinists. They were joking about the effect caused by a minor second in a symphony by Manfredini. The oldest of them, who had been first violinist under the conductor Theodor Fuchs, helped him with his crutches so that he could lie down. Because of his illness they had set up a bed of sorts raised some

twenty centimetres above the floor and made from some
wooden planks stolen during a concert in the Faculty of
Law. The youngest of the six, who was forty-two, offered
Triclinio a bowl of soup and told him that if he wished he
could stay and join their orchestra. "Here you will have
no homeland, but no master either," he assured him in
all earnestness. Triclinio tried to express his gratitude
but could not find the words. Then the youngest of the
arthritics playfully called him a foolish and sentimental
provincial: "When you came here you were not chasing
the song of the birds but the legs of the factory girls.
Tomorrow I'll take you to the neighbourhood around
the fingerboard where there are some gorgeous social
workers."

11

Farewell to the city

Violinville was separated from Buenos Aires and from
the rest of the country by a putrid river whose waters,
which were full of organic refuse, served to irrigate the
trees that the arthritic violinists grew in their garden.

If music was not exactly the core of their existence,
they nevertheless used it as a form of escape, a code
or constitution which they all loved equally so as to
avoid the complications of jealousy. They had created
a sense of equilibrium among themselves which went
as unobserved as the freedom they enjoyed. Each of
them was free to do as he wished; this appeared to
be their motto, and in this way they discovered many
different forms of happiness. Just as they had built their
own instruments, specially adapted to their arthritis, so
they also composed their own music, which reflected a
freedom so feared by others. They made no use of the
stave in their compositions, but they did not reject it,
and it featured in some of the avant-garde compositions
of the younger, more daring composers. To be able to
play these works, each musician jotted his themes in
any language that took his fancy, using, among other
things, drawings, numerals, balls, spheres, wires, nails
and horseshoes. The last of these were also used as
instruments. Since all of the violinists played, they were
also their own audience, and were therefore spared the

ordeal of dealing with innocents or a tiresome following of fanatics. They played on the main street which, like all the streets in the town, was also an allotment, and in moments of deep inspiration, they often gathered ears of corn or pumpkins to produce sound effects which nourished their soaring spirits. Their instruments, while respecting the classical division of pitch, were made from the most varied materials – paraffin drums, old bottles, lead piping, gourds, the casings of tear-gas grenades, dogs and cats (live), the odd bird, horse-flies, tubes of toothpaste, wooden planks, spare parts of motor cars, newspaper cuttings – texts for cantatas and madrigals – boots and hand-bells. One very important instrument, the most expensive of all should they have had to buy it, was the train which passed at fixed times and which they invariably introduced into their compositions. Sadly, planes and helicopters, much valued by the arthritics, could not be included, for the state of siege made their comings and goings unpredictable.

Vegetarians by circumstance rather than conviction, they did not reject the rare piece of meat that chanced to come their way. Intestines were not eaten but used as strings for their instruments. Therefore the temporary ban on beef which sparked off proclamations, debates, announcements in the press and even disorders in the streets, from which they were protected by the river, did not affect them. To be without meat became part of the free existence they had chosen to pursue.

The orchestra rehearsed regularly within the schedule they had set themselves. Sometimes, according to the season, they confused night with day, so that they might well be practising before dawn, while on the other side of the river Buenos Aires imagined itself asleep. On these occasions, the nicest part was that the train passed when least expected and the sudden noise produced surprising sound effects which gave them enormous pleasure.

As for their political organization, since the general interest was simply general, no one had to watch over it or act on its behalf, except as a form of punishment – the only punishment practised in Violinville. If during a rehearsal (or concert, for they were one and the same thing) anyone tuned up in the classical manner, he was automatically elected mayor for the day, and given the responsibility of seeing that the roads were swept and the town kept clean. He also had to look after the social workers and to enquire of each of them how things were going, only ever to be given the angry reply: "What things?" or "Who asked you to meddle in our affairs?" For that day he became the most unpopular fellow in the town, but once he had served his time he went back to playing in the manner of free men. They had all been mayor for a day at some time or other, for musicians too can err.

Since they were neither hospitable nor hostile, Triclinio was readily accepted by the town's inhabitants, without obligations or rights, except for those which arose from the transparency of the atmosphere. Triclinio adapted to this situation immediately, unlike Ufa, who, although she was accepted by all and often visited the town, tried to indoctrinate the inhabitants from time to time with trite phrases which indicated that she frequented the Colon, a place they regarded as metaphysical hell. Yet no one ever reproached Ufa or refused to listen to her descriptions of the concerts in that theatre of banal musical games. The elderly inhabitants smiled at her descriptions, and the less elderly positively revelled in them.

When Triclinio was able to walk without using crutches, the first thing he did was to cross the river and go to Buenos Aires in search of his violin and other belongings. Feeling a little apprehensive, he wandered through the streets, bidding farewell to the city which had everything yet had given him nothing. He gazed at the pretty girls in their summer dresses, the pensioners enjoying the sunshine on park benches, the restaurants displaying a wide choice of meat dishes, the shop windows filled with useless, imported goods, the anchored ships dreaming of remote lands, the children who were on their way to school to learn about Argentina's history – the children who were the hope of the future – the people rushing in and out of the subway stations, at the same breathtaking speed with which they spoke, the Ministry for the Navy, the Chase Manhattan Bank, the sun filtering through the trees in Lezama Park, the police communications headquarters, the latest issue of the comic book *Patoruzu of the Pampas*, the French hardware store, the King of Ravioli, the Mitre Museum and many other landmarks he had come to cherish in the city. Before crossing the river to return to Violinville, he took one last nostalgic look at the presidential palace where his friend the President had been destroyed by radio propaganda. If he should ever chance to run into him, he would present him with a picture of the Virgin of Lujan.

He returned to Violinville full of optimism and feeling lively as a young colt. Under his arm he carried the precious violin of San Francisco Solano which he would put at the disposal of all his friends, in particular the six violinists with whom he shared a room. The latter gave him a welcoming nod without interrupting their singing as they finished assembling a musical instrument of immense complexity made from pipes and sheet-metal taken from a derailed train. They had started to assemble it inside the room without knowing how large it would be once it was finished. Then, when it almost covered the entire floor of the room, they carried it out onto the street so that, in addition to being an instrument, it might also serve as a monument to one of the shantytown's secret heroes.

The least arthritic of the six violinists explained to Triclinio that the instrument they had just assembled belonged to the family of wind instruments. Indeed, amidst its intricate structure there was a little tube one could blow through. The arthritic in the middle pointed out: "The only apparent problem, and I say apparent because this is a particular feature which makes the instrument so beautiful and effective, is the complexity of its acoustic mechanism, made with bits of rail. It has to be blown for several hours before the concert, because the sound makes numerous detours before it exits at the other end. The thing to remember is to blow at the right moment so that the sound will come out when required by the score. There is one further advantage. As well as being both instrument and monument, it is also something of a joke and makes people happy. Isn't it marvellous? Now let's have a look at your conventional instrument."

Not one of the six arthritics could play Triclinio's real violin. The arthritic in the middle said that the only way they could possibly manage with their deformed fingers would be to play on the side of the fingerboard. "It would be interesting to add another fingerboard onto the side where we could rest our fingers and then the real strings would be able to produce a sort of echo, and we would have a lovely viola d'amore. You must take it to the maestro."

The great maestro examined and measured the instrument and saw that it coincided perfectly with the line, weight and desideratum of his imaginary violin. In his opinion it was a fine instrument. One simply had to play it at the side where no fingerboard existed. "In any case, if Triclinio so wished, he could play this violin at tomorrow's concert. Let's see if this will rouse the hopelessly prudish social workers," he said before going back to the instrument which he carried everywhere.

12

The amazing concert of the arthritics

The musicians-cum-audience had assembled in Finger-board Avenue — the town's main street — to begin the *Concerto for two inner tubes and tear-gas*, this time with the participation of a traditional violin to be played by Triclinio.

"We have chosen this work," one of the arthritics explained, "because it drives the social workers into a frenzy, especially in the section where we really tune our instruments and the inner tubes make some splendid scales in descending thirds. When the social workers arrive, feel free to choose the one you prefer, then at least one of them will get what she's looking for and you will get what you fancy."

The wind section had been enriched by the participation of a number of children with large balloons which they inflated during the moments of silence. As the balloons were deflated, they produced sounds and timbres which were truly Vivaldian.

Most of the children were the offspring of the social workers who had decided to learn about the problems of the arthritic violinists by sharing their lives. As wives, they were integrated into the violinists' culture. Their children, however, were normal — with none of the occupational illnesses of their mothers and without arthritis.

The concert had started informally with the crowing of cockerels and the din of noisy exhausts in nearby Buenos Aires. The instrument-cum-statue had been duly blown the previous day by one of the six violinists, and the sounds were travelling through the complicated tubes and acoustic bends constructed from the pipes of a railway heating system. The group of six were to use instruments made from Yale keys and tubes of tranquillizers found on a rubbish dump in the city. The piece they were playing, however, had only five parts, so the most arthritic of the six violinists infused some maté leaves and chatted with the others during the frequent pauses in the score. Triclinio had been given a violin solo which he was free to introduce whenever he wished, although they recommended that he should try to play off the notes, if possible in fourths or octaves, except in the passage played in descending scales on inner tubes and dedicated to the social workers; there, to achieve a truly classical effect, he should play conventional notes.

Towards midday, right in the middle of the second movement, the women who were not playing, or who had momentarily stopped, brought in a dish of birds' eggs and sweet corn. After they had eaten and the inner tubes had played the cadenza, one of the six suggested to Triclinio that he should play his solo during the siesta so that anyone who wished to sleep could do so to the rhythm of sweet, exotic music.

Three blue balloons marked his entrance and Triclinio began to play off the notes, although he made a surprising number of mistakes for someone whose right hand was quite sound. As had been predicted, Triclinio's playing caught the attention of the social workers, and no fewer than sixty of them rushed forward, startled by this phenomenon which could threaten the precious tranquillity enjoyed by the inhabitants of Violinville.

While many of the musicians were bored by the mawkish solemnity of Triclinio's solo, others slept harmoniously, reclining against their instruments under a lukewarm sun whose spots had almost disappeared. These sun-spots were a matter of some importance, for whenever they increased everyone knew that disorders were breaking out again in Buenos Aires and in the other large cities in the country. A little old man who was unwittingly eating his instrument – a scooped-out melon – explained that the sun-spots "sometimes change our plans, for we are children of the sun, are we not?"

Triclinio barely heard him speak. He was too overcome by the presence of the social workers who were staring at him and listening attentively as they frantically consulted their manuals. Triclinio's handsome face with its Indian traits, olive skin and eyes which turned green from drinking so much maté tea, and the sounds coming from his violin clearly overwhelmed these impressionable social workers, who stared at him in amazement, sometimes as if he were a madman, at other times as if he were a flower.

"Which one of them do you prefer?" asked the musician who was infusing the maté.

"All of them," replied Triclinio.

Then an arthritic handed him twenty quavers made from stolen railway copper and told him to throw them one by one to the social workers.

They were all extremely beautiful, with sensuous, feline eyes and long flowing hair. The poorest of them, almost genuine inhabitants of Violinville, wore expensive costumes provided by Ufa from the wardrobes of the Colon, costumes originally designed for operas no longer in the repertoire. Other wore transparent garments made of paper, while others, naked as mermaids, exposed their burnished skin as creatures of the sun. They smiled affably as Triclinio threw the copper quavers. They did not stir, each hoping to be the target of one of them. At that moment a quaver hit the social worker Palmira in the face, whereupon the musicians and other social workers cried out joyfully: "Hail the future bride." Palmira lowered her eyes, bashful in the face of this nascent love. She snuggled at Triclinio's feet, ready to become his betrothed the moment he finished playing his violin solo which he had interrupted to throw the copper quavers.

The orchestra then improvised a lively wedding march which the cats and dogs joined with great gusto.

Having finished his part, Triclinio put down his violin and began to caress Palmira, whose laughter was as harmonious as a sweet tenor flute. "A kiss, a kiss," the orchestra now sang in the form of a choral canon, but at this moment a series of explosions could be heard coming from the city nearby, which caused the Yale keys, the three thousand tubes of tranquillizers and the wire quavers hanging on the pink walls of the room of the six violinists to clang furiously. Suddenly a column of smoke coming from the Plaza de Mayo rose up into the sky, as if the Colon itself were in flames. Then there was the sound of machine-guns, followed by the explosion of tear-gas grenades, the merest fraction of a second earlier than the timings marked in the scores. Triclinio questioned Palmira, who was purring at his side, and she explained that it was part of the work they were playing. "It's the part I like best because it is so harmonious," she said, revealing her knowledge of music reviews in the newspapers.

A lorry filled with busts of deposed presidents drove by and tipped them into the lagoon. Many were made of bronze, so they could be used to make wind instruments. The sound of speeches, marching, tanks, statues being wrenched from their pedestals and later replaced, could also be heard. The arthritics explained that this was the second part of the concert, as they went on playing their tubes and keys. Palmira added didactically that if all this constituted the second part of the concert, it was a truly historic event, at least in the figurative sense of the word. "They are reaching some agreement and this is a good sign," she concluded, enveloping Triclinio with a voluptuous look.

Dusk was falling over Buenos Aires, and the clouds of tear-gas merged in the sky with the fumes of the cars and factories, but in Violinville the generous sun was still casting its last rays of light.

The orchestra now launched into a special arrangement of Albinoni's adagio for instrument-cum-statue and strings. Palmira, realizing that it was getting late, insisted that she must go home at once to prepare her trousseau because the wedding was to take place that same evening. One of her companions had offered her an old costume from a production of *Madame Butterfly* that would go well with Triclinio's alpaca poncho, which was frayed by the infectious diseases in La Rioja and the humid climate of the capital.

This was what they were discussing when Ufa's gondola appeared at the Buenos Aires end of the lagoon. Preceded by fireworks, it was like some magical apparition. The musicians received Ufa with percussion, strings and cries of joy, for she always came laden with gifts: bomb casings, used bullets, programmes of classical music and the occasional pigeon from the Plaza de Mayo.

When Ufa disembarked, all the musicians stopped playing and gathered round to see what pretty things she had brought them this time. She distributed as best she could the knick-knacks that she extracted from large baskets filled with flowers, newspaper editorials, copies of the latest decrees, empty boxes, horseshoes, handsaws, hooters taken from official government cars, tiny bronze stars, harnesses, a white horse and thousands of other objects which everyone could use as they saw fit. When they had with warm embraces expressed their gratitude for the gifts, she took the horse by its bridle and, going up to Triclinio, she told him:

"I have heard all about your plight from the workers at the thread factory who survived. This horse, stolen from the army stables, will always provide you with the horsehairs you need for your violin bow, which they tell me makes the most wonderful sound. Give me the card which classifies you as a *displaced* person, a euphemism for *exiled*, and I'll give you another in exchange classifying you as a *visitor under observation*. You are a guest, aren't you? With this card, you will be able to return to Buenos Aires and you will see just how much you and I together will achieve."

With mixed feelings of relief and bewilderment, Triclinio was about to reply when the instrument-cum-statue blared out unexpectedly and without any orchestral accompaniment. This provoked an outburst of laughter, singing and shouting, which lasted until dawn.

It was a curious scale of sounds situated somewhere between a fife, a bassoon and a railway disaster. Through some hole in the pipe came shrill sounds, peep-peep, which disturbed the toads in the lagoon.

Beneath Ufa's chignon one could perceive long braided tresses, and her forehead was adorned with little flowers and haloed with spangles. Her steady gaze appeared to belong to another world, and it never left Triclinio, who was shy, and was caught between stroking his horse and stroking Ufa.

The lukewarm sun could be glimpsed through the carbon monoxide as Ufa told Triclinio that she needed his assistance and, turning to the six violinists, explained that Triclinio would only be gone for a few hours.

They boarded the gondola and then disappeared towards the horizon of skyscrapers. Seated on a bench in the little square to the left of the bridge, Palmira, with lowered head, was sewing her trousseau. But because of her tears she could not see to thread the needle.

13

Ufa's curious pedigree

Once inside the gondola, Ufa let down her hair and changed into a simple Mao jacket which also served as a mini-shift. She put on some lipstick, so that the breeze coming from the river would not chap her lips, then, looking at Triclinio dressed in his poncho and lost in thought, said: "You're good-looking. I'll bet the social workers never leave you in peace." Triclinio, who was still clutching his violin, gave her an enigmatic smile. He thought to himself that Ufa was as beautiful as the effigy of Liberty on the old ten-centavo coins; all she needed was a Phrygian cap.

On the opposite shore of the lagoon, some seventy policemen on motorcycles – not to mention those hidden in the gondola – were waiting for Ufa. After helping her to alight, all of them trained their sub-machine-guns on Triclinio. "He's with me," she said, whereupon the policemen lowered their weapons. The policeman who seemed to be in charge saluted Triclinio. A little old man, looking as if he had stepped straight out of an opera by Verdi, ushered them into a car, and, with sirens wailing, they set off at full speed for the city centre, followed by the seventy motorcyclists.

Triclinio was blocking his ears when he suddenly heard Ufa whisper: "Now you can kiss me." When he replied that he did not feel like kissing her, she told him: "You can't imagine how relieved I am. There is something rather vulgar about kissing inside a car."

During this deafening journey, she told him that she liked swimming, dancing, target practice, yoga and horse-riding, and she studied German folk culture and political economy. "And I adore the people of Violinville and consider it my duty to help them. Mummy and daddy will be delighted to meet you."

They arrived at a distinguished-looking suburban villa. The car and motorcycles disappeared into the gardens. The villa itself was divided into two parts, the one illuminated, the other in darkness. In the darkened part, the walls were covered with ancient and modern weapons, ranging from blunderbusses used in the Wars of Independence to automatic pistols fitted with silencers. In the illuminated part, on the other hand, there were thousands of shining objects which had been meticulously arranged, and everything smelled of cleanliness, detergent and disinfectant. Both parts of the villa were connected by a single door, bare on one side, and covered with guns on the other.

"This villa," said Ufa, by way of a prologue, "was specially built for my parents. The problem is that daddy likes collecting guns and spends his weekends greasing them one by one. Before we came to live here, mummy, who adores cleanliness, especially since she discovered the existence of detergents, sprinkled water over daddy's weapons which made them go rusty. Since this would be grounds for divorce in any civilized country, an architect friend of ours designed this house with one wing for cleaning and the other for collecting guns. Peace has now been restored to our household, despite my father's hobby. This is a room with old musical instruments.

There are seventeen violins among other items, But let's go and look somewhere else, because with your friends from Violinville, I suspect you've had enough of music. Daddy played the violin quite well before his present job. Now the poor man works all day and he has so many worries he has scarcely enough time to grease his blunderbusses. You will see how kind daddy is once you get to know him. He is nothing like the man who appears on television. Daddy is also very fond of the people of Violinville but he has been trained in the classical repertoire and he says he will never be able to understand their music. Those musicians, believe me, are not quite as naïve as they seem. Sometimes they get their scores to Buenos Aires using all sorts of cunning strategies, which in all innocence the orchestras then play, disconcerting the critics, the intelligence services, and the secret police, because no one employed by these agencies knows anything about experimental music. Daddy does, though – he even corresponds with John Cage – and he would have banned such music at once. Thanks to my friendship with the people of Violinville, I always know in advance when this subversive music is going to be played and I can persuade daddy that he is suffering from migraine and must stay home. Time and time again, I have warned your six friends responsible for this music to stop sending their subversive works to the Colon. But all they do is put on angelic looks, tell me they are innocent, and then bombard me with hemidemisemiquavers made of wire because they all want to marry me. That's how it's been so far, but we are still good friends. You must understand that I have no desire to stop their games, even though they might get them into trouble with the authorities. I simply want to protect them from being found out and sprayed with that foul coloured water which makes their arthritis worse and ruins their houses."

From there they passed into an attic covered in dust, where they found, stored among the clutter, war trophies which had belonged to Ufa's ancestors, tattered flags, pieces of shrapnel, a copy of the National Constitution and a portrait of Che.

"This is daddy's den. He shuts himself away in here in order to work out really difficult problems. I have seen him trembling from head to foot, so I don't like him being in here. When he shuts himself away in the attic, mummy cries and she calls his den the second-hand shop."

"Back in my native province," Triclinio told Ufa, "they arrested a carpenter friend of mine, took him to Buenos Aires and locked him up on a ship because he kept a banner with a portrait of Che in his house. Isn't your father also in danger of being arrested?"

Ufa smiled as the effigy of Liberty on the old ten-centavo coins might have smiled. Then she said:

"Daddy is a wonderful man. He might even have left-wing sympathies. Who knows? But some things, very few, he doesn't understand, and others he refuses to accept. I once asked him if he supported the left, when I discovered this portrait of Che hidden away, and he told me he could never support the left because all its members are wicked. But I can assure you that, deep down, daddy does understand. He simply likes to see everything in its right place, like those guns of his, which are all arranged according to their age and firepower. Do you have a girlfriend?"

"No," Triclinio lied, thinking of Palmira and searching for something to say. But Ufa, taking a deep breath and looking at him against the light, went on speaking.

"In the world you have chosen at Violinville, love is as normal as arthritis or experimental music. The happiness those musicians enjoy in exile is even more enhanced by love. Living in exile, they carry no burden on their shoulders, and they are not accountable either to history or for the destiny of their homeland. Because Argentina, despite everything, is a nation, isn't it? Here in the house, we preserve the weapons which our grandfathers used to defend our frontiers, and there's a family album which will bowl you over. Would you like to read the letters Chacho Peñaloza wrote to my great-grandfather? Or would you prefer to see the death certificate of Felipe Varela? Or the letters that Facundo Quiroga wrote in English — for heaven's sake — to my aunt's cousin? Do you see? La Rioja isn't all there is to this country, my darling, although you might not think so. Many things have happened here too. To come to grips with the past requires such abnegation of self that not even yoga will save you. Have you any idea of the sacrifices my ancestors made during the reconquest of Buenos Aires at the time of the English invasions? Or of what they endured under the first military dictator, Juan Manuel de Rosas? Do you know anything about Manuel Dorrego, the martyr of Independence? About the corpse of that other hero of the campaign for Independence, Lavalle, abandoned at the bottom of the Humahuaca ravine? About the Banderita Treaty, signed in May 1862? About the international pressures, about meat rationing, about banking problems, about how to set up a constitution? Or, going a little further back, are you interested in knowing something about the meeting between our heroes in the fight for Independence at Guayaquil in 1822? Or perhaps you'd be interested in the question of the repatriation of the mortal remains of

Rosas? Or maybe, since you're looking so mournfully nostalgic, you'd like to know what became of Eva Peron's corpse, like those hopeless fanatics who believe she was shot. And all you are likely to get from knowing all this," she added, close to tears, "is that you may be accused of being frivolous and bourgeois."

Triclinio was about to reply, troubled by the twilight crimson which had crept into Ufa's cheeks, reminding him of the description of the dictator's beautiful daughter, Manuelita Rosas, as she emerged from church and distributed alms to the poor in the radio serial which his father used to listen to, but before he could utter a word, Ufa, who had calmed down a little, was already speaking:

"I'm glad you didn't kiss me in the car or try to take liberties like all the others do. Nine colonels and a whole regiment of generals have proposed, plus a whole bevy of second lieutenants. But love has to be earned, my darling, just as you finally earned your violin after studying like mad for ten long years."

Triclinio picked up a violin he saw lying on a table and plucked a few strings. "That's mummy's violin. It had quite a nice tone until she cleaned it with alcohol and you can see what happened then. And now do me a favour and get changed. You will find some clothes over there. I am going to take you to a concert at the Colon.

While Triclinio got into evening dress, Ufa, taking another deep breath, continued:

"Love must not be treated as if it were a free gift or a bonus, just as it is impossible to restore the nation's economy with a decree. I must tell you, I don't like to see you getting mixed up with that social worker. They are always chasing after innocents like you. I dare say that they mean well but I think you deserve something better. After being defeated in the civil wars, your province has been neglected for a long time. Daddy always speaks of La Rioja with affection. Although I'm very fond of you, I shall only be able to love you when the country regains some stability and that strikes me as being extremely unlikely, if not impossible. Don't think that the differences between us are too great just because you have seen the treasures in this house and because of daddy's position. Mummy's origins are even more humble than your own, and that's why she has this mania for hygiene and even tried to clean a violin with alcohol. But daddy succeeded in bringing her up to his level with lots of patience and affection, and now the only place she refuses to go to is the Colon. Otherwise she accompanies him everywhere. And now put out the light, no, the candle, stupid, for we are off to the theatre."

14

Triclinio savours glory

On the corner of Cerrito there was a long queue of fans waiting for autographs. They had been there for many hours, munching sandwiches, preparing meals on handy little braziers or grilling pieces of meat at the kerbside.

There was a performance of *Rigoletto* and the theatre was full. Ufa nodded politely to acknowledge the salutes of the military and civilian police, but instead of entering the family box she headed straight for the front stalls so that Triclinio might have a good view of the entire auditorium.

"This place is rather old-fashioned," she told him, "but you saw the queue along Cerrito Street. Your friends think that this theatre is some kind of musical brothel, but the place has a certain charm. It is part of the nation's history, one of its myths, like Carlitos Gardel's tango, or Libertad Lamarque, or a *coup d'état.*"

"*Rigoletto*," Triclinio spelled out.

"Yes: but I haven't the faintest idea who's singing. According to my grandfather, who knows a great deal about opera, no performance has ever reached the heights of the gala evening in 1910 which, as you must know, was the centenary of Argentine independence, when Graciela Pareto, Tita Ruffa and Giuseppe Anselmi, all international stars, sang in the presence of the Infanta Isabel, representing the King of Spain. My grandfather knew the vengeance duet by heart, but even though he had a good voice, he could never reach the baritone G."

Triclinio, looking up at the ceiling, said, "Very pretty," and then, "What a fine La," as the orchestra began tuning up.

Since Triclinio had made it clear that he did not know the plot of this or any other opera and that he had never been to a performance, Ufa explained the plot of *Rigoletto*. He was greatly amused. "It's just like the strip cartoons in the magazines my father used to receive from Buenos Aires in exchange for his honey."

When the artists began to sing in Italian, Ufa gave Triclinio a questioning look. He reassured her that he could understand most of what they were singing because his violin teacher Spumarola used to chide him in Italian during his violin lessons. Triclinio tried to show some interest in the opera, but found it quite absurd.

"Do you like it, Triclinio?"

"More or less. The trouble is, I can't understand a word the soprano is singing."

"You know why, don't you? The situation has become intolerable. Artistic policy lays down that the soloists should be foreigners, but Europe is vast, and this soprano is singing in Russian – an impossible language – because she doesn't know the role in Italian. Don't be surprised to find that some of them even sing in French. Fortunately, the audience knows the opera from beginning to end – *Rigoletto* has been performed here regularly since 1908 – and so everyone knows the story."

Triclinio folded and unfolded his programme and kept looking up at the ceiling.

"You're bored, eh? You're wonderful! Daddy says that El Peludo also found opera boring. Do you know who El

Peludo was? No? That's incredible. He was a founder of
the Radical Party and held the same political views as
your maestro Spumarola. A grocer's son who rose to
become president of the Argentine Republic. He always
had that box over there on the gala evenings for the
anniversary of independence. But he hated music and
the gentry would leave the auditorium the moment he
arrived. He used to yawn when the divas sang their arias,
and his daughter Elena once had the nerve to serve meat
pies in the presidential box. Can you imagine? Another
time he insisted that the Egyptian high priests had to
sing the National Anthem in the second act of *Aida*. It
was so incredibly coarse that the presidential guards,
who had travelled to the theatre by tram, would not even
salute him."

Triclinio laughed so heartily at the thought of
presidential guards travelling by tram that several
elderly ladies peered at him aghast from their boxes.

"Be quiet. You're not in Violinville," Ufa cautioned
him, amused and alarmed at the same time.

Just as Ufa had predicted, two singers performed their
duet, one singing in Italian, the other in French, and this
provoked another outburst of laughter from Triclinio.

Ufa smiled condescendingly, and began to speak as if
to herself:

"Really, things are going from bad to worse. Of course,
the next leader of the Radical Party, Marcelo, was a
marvellous man. That was the best time of all for this
nation and this theatre. All the foreign singers who came
here knew Marcelo because, although he was governor of
this country, he had actually lived in Paris when he was
Ambassador. Anyway, he always patronized the Colon
and even married a Portuguese soprano, Regina, who
often came to sing at our house after he had forbidden

her to sing in public and had smashed all her records.
I was only a little girl at the time, but I remember her
singing an aria from *I Puritani* in the room where
daddy keeps his guns now. I suppose you do realize that
I'm talking about President Marcelo Alvear. Marcelo
was such a darling. He used to spend every summer in
Mar del Plata wearing pyjamas and solving the nation's
problems in between Pernods. And Argentina was never
better. He really knew how to live it up. Your Peludo,
on the other hand, forbade Josephine Baker to appear
dancing in the nude. Can you imagine anyone being so
reactionary? Thank goodness. It's the interval. Let's go
to the foyer. The programme says that they are about to
give the first performance of a new opera by a modern
composer. I think he's Australian. Are you enjoying
yourself? Did you ever imagine that you would be in
the Colon for the première of an opera by an Australian
composer?"

Discreetly followed by eight presidential guards, four
federal policemen and other unidentified agents, Ufa
and Triclinio sipped a sherry of indifferent quality. At
every turn they were greeted obsequiously by important
people: stock-breeders, grain merchants, ambassadors
and irascible industrialists. Ufa gave a different smile to
each of them, as she clung to Triclinio, who drew
extraordinary greetings in view of his unexpected
presence and appearance. Standing before a mirror,
Triclinio examined his evening dress, his shoes, his eyes,
his hair sleek and stoical, his chin almost heroic, the
shape of his head positively dolichocephalic. Observing
out of the corner of his eye that Ufa was staring at him
fascinated, he told himself that Spumarola's predictions
were about to come true, and that from this moment he
was about to fulfil that destiny so much awaited and

desired by all the great musicians whose biographies he had read in the magazines sent in exchange for the secret labours of his father's prophetic bees.

15

A most bizarre opera

After the interval and a few drinks which consoled Triclinio's Montonero heart, came the one-act opera by the Australian composer. Ufa felt a little uneasy because she had been warned by the intelligence services that something strange was about to happen in the Colon that evening.

Her nervousness gave her an air of even greater beauty, and Triclinio, who had been absorbed in studying her inch by inch, found her truly delicious.

"Would you like to know something," Triclinio said. "You have the loveliest eyes."

"Please, Tricly," she answered. She was looking attentively at the costume of the two soloists who had come on stage. One was a kangaroo, the other a platypus. "What horrible creatures," Ufa said.

A number of policemen in plain clothes dashed up to the front row, while others armed with tear-gas guns, took up positions in the boxes nearby. After the overture, a curious piece of orchestration with the oddest symbols in the middle of the notes (the musicians were playing the score for the first time), the kangaroo sang in a tenor voice:

I am a kangaroo
tu ay tu ay

I live on grass
tu ay tu ay
When I take a jump
tu ay tu ay
I hold my breath tu ay tu ay

The platypus, in a harsh treble voice, replied:

Platypus
tu ay tu ay
bird and bill
tu ay tu ay
I look odd
tu ay tu ay
but I am mammal tu ay tu ay

The kangaroo:

You are mammal
tu ay tu ay
a cross between a duck
and a load of shit
you are mammal
tu ay tu ay
but without any nipples tu ay tu ay

The platypus:

You have a pouch
tu ay tu ay
and eat grass
tu ay tu ay
and your swollen pubes

tu ay tu ay
are quite revolting tu ay tu ay

The kangaroo:

I find you disgusting
tu ay tu ay
with that psittacosis
tu ay tu ay
which contaminates
our lungs tu ay tu ay

The platypus:

Hairy beast
tu ay tu ay
degenerate species
tu ay tu ay
only the parrots
tu ay tu ay
have psittacosis tu ay tu ay

"This reminds me of the gaucho singing contest between Martin Fierro and El Moreno," Triclinio commented.

The kangaroo:

I stuff your nonsense
tu ay tu ay
in my pouch
tu ay tu ay
I might be hairy
tu ay tu ay
but your bum is bare tu ay tu ay

"This is becoming offensive," Ufa exclaimed, looking towards the proscenium; "I think we should move quietly to the back of the theatre. It looks as if things could turn nasty."

Musically, the soloists were now singing such a beautiful duet that they remained in their seats a few more seconds.

The duet between the kangaroo and the platypus:

For after all
tu ay tu ay
we come from Australia
tu ay tu ay
inhabited land
tu ay tu ay
colonized by Spain tu ay tu ay

"I knew it. Politics! Your friends are responsible for this. Those six violinists. I'd know their work anywhere. This is not the first time they've smuggled in scores and those stupid musicians and their fool of a conductor can't see what's going on under their very noses. Now because of their little prank we'll all have to put up with another cloud of tear-gas."

The duet continued:

And then
tu ay tu ay
the English arrived
two I two I
the English arrived
and stole our boomerang

The first gas grenade landed right between the kangaroo and the platypus, followed by jets of multicoloured water. Ufa was indignant and tried to speak to the policeman who was giving orders, but she could not make herself heard above the uproar.

The soloists went on singing as if nothing had happened, even though they were no longer accompanied by the orchestra, for the musicians had fled in disarray along with the audience.

"Let's get out of here." Ufa caught Triclinio by the poncho. "Didn't I tell you this place is no longer fashionable?"

From the doorway they heard the final stanza:

Anyhow
tu ay tu ay
we have a Queen
tu ay tu ay
and Sydney Harbour
tu ay tu ay
and even an Antarctica like Argentina tu ay tu ay

After eating at a nearby pizzeria, Ufa's anger subsided, her cheeks were no longer flushed and she looked as fresh and delicious as ever.

"I have to admit it," she said, "daddy was right. Things are getting out of hand. I had thought of inviting you home to dinner but now daddy will almost certainly have a migraine and he won't be in a mood for visitors. For the time being, my darling, you had better rejoin your friends. Here are the papers I promised, and if you want you can even have an audience with the president."

She gave him a sisterly peck on the cheek, then walked away in the direction of the Plaza de Mayo, looking despondent.

16

Il Trillo del Diavolo

The president sat at the far end of the audience chamber. Invisible loudspeakers transmitted piped music based on a theme by Telemann with which Triclinio was familiar. When he got closer, he saw that the president had a kind expression and he began to think that all the things he had heard and read about tortures, stories which had spread even to Brazil, were nothing but lies.

"Please sit down," the president said, extending a handshake and, after he had glanced through Triclinio's papers, he continued: "I see from your file that you turned down all openings in local industries in your native province in order to take up the violin upon the advice of one of the leaders of the Radical Party. Then you abandoned La Rioja, where violinists are not in demand, obviously, and came to Buenos Aires where almost everyone plays the violin. So now you will have to go on perfecting your art beyond all perfection in order to make a living, and that will be extremely difficult if not impossible. The violin, like the nation itself, has become so complicated in recent years because of a handful of neurotics. Things being as they are, all too few reach that perfection of technique which would ensure success. But the only way to succeed is to go through a lengthy and rigorous apprenticeship. Don't you agree?"

"Yes sir," Triclinio replied, but an aide cautioned him that he should only speak when formally addressed. The president went on:

"Now then, we must ask you a few questions, only a formality to add to your file."

A minister or someone of that order approached with a sheet of paper and began to fire questions at Triclinio in a Buenos Aires dialect which he could barely understand, although he found it most pleasing to the ear.

"Do you know how to ride a horse? How to type? How to handle a machine-gun, a 15.5 calibre howitzer, a Molotov cocktail, an electric prod? No. Can you drive a lorry or tractor, handle a police dog or a water cannon? No. Well, what about a Peronist demonstration, a trade union law, a Ministry for Economic Affairs, a wheelbarrow? No. That will be all, thank you. It seems clear enough that the only thing you are capable of doing is playing the violin, and that still has to be proved."

The president raised one eyebrow as a signal for the official to sit down and be quiet, and then said ambiguously:

"You strike me as being the type of chap who came broken into this world with *worn-out tools*, to quote Rudyard Kipling. Your main concern and function is to play your thirds as well as possible and to obtain a sound that is not only beautiful and pure but also convincing, all of which requires daily exercises that may sometimes seem to reduce life to nothing but conditioned reflexes. But don't let it worry you. I am only saying all this in order that we can have a frank discussion. After all, you are surviving, are you not? That is what matters. In my opinion, the violin is an unnatural instrument, like alchemy, invented by the government's opponents to attain the absolute by a progressive mastery of technique. It is absurd. In the end all that remains is the symbol, that fine, esoteric instrument which you are holding in your hands."

The president, his features flushed with benevolence, raised an eyebrow signal to an aide standing nearby, who pressed a button on the president's desk. This resulted in Triclinio's fingerprints being projected onto the wall.

"There you see," the statesman continued, "that you are unable to reason because your head is filled with sounds. Don't be frightened or imagine that this is something new or abnormal. This country, as I've always tried to say, is being invaded by sounds to prevent us from understanding reality. And if we do not see it we cannot confront it. What this government fears most is not that people should be unable to understand reality but that they should choose not to understand. You can switch it off now." He swallowed and added: "Come what may, we need beauty in order to exist, for beauty is the human dimension of reality."

The effort of composing this aphorism obliged him to pause. Then he solemnly declared: "This is what the inhabitants of your native Rioja do not understand, and that's why you have no future there as a violinist. But let me tell you that the meat traders and grain merchants of Buenos Aires do not understand it either. For them the violin is nothing but a way of overcoming spleen. What we are trying to do is to reconcile the two hypotheses, and we are ready to suppress by force those who would oppose us. Do you understand? I should also make it clear before you start playing that I know you are the proud owner of the violin that once belonged to San Francisco Solano. Have no fear, we shall not let on. For many years we have had to keep many more important secrets. And now I should like you to play for me."

After tuning the second string, Triclinio looked at the president as if seeking approval. The latter assented with a nod and said: "That's a fine La; I like it."

Triclinio was about to start playing when he felt the building shake. At first, because of his provincial naïvety, he thought it was the carpet moving, but, listening more carefully, he realized that the building was indeed shaking although this might not have been perceptible to someone who had no ear for music. The president's ear, also finely tuned, alerted him and he looked questioningly at his aides who had heard nothing and decided that the alleged tremor would disappear with the music.

Triclinio rose to his feet and vigorously launched into the *Romanza* by Sarasate. The acoustics in the audience chamber were sheer bliss. The president, captivated by the music, closed his eyes and succumbed to sweet hallucinations. His ministers, on the other hand, remained upright, with their eyes fixed on the luminous teleprinter standing discreetly in a corner, which gave the prices quoted on the meat market and the ups and downs of the dollar exchange rate. One of these prices alarmed the president's aides but, exchanging knowing looks among themselves, they decided not to disturb the president who was swaying his head to the rhythmic fluctuations of the *Romanza*.

When Triclinio performed this work without piano accompaniment, he could hear in his mind, as he finished, that final chord on the piano, *tan*. But he was not given enough time to hear it for, as soon as he had finished playing the violin part, someone at his shoulder called out *tan*, playing the piano chord. When he turned round to look, the girl who had intoned the chord put out her tongue affectionately, a tongue as pink and pretty as her face. "Wonderful! Divine! You play like a god," she exclaimed.

It was Ufa, dressed in her official uniform and looking like an eighteen-year-old, with a golden complexion and long pigtails. The same Ufa as ever, yet even more beautiful and natural than when she was at home or in Violinville, despite the solemn surroundings in which they both found themselves. The dignity of power, far from giving her the military air of the *March of San Lorenzo*, became transformed in Ufa into the pensive serenity of the lilies of the field: like an acacia or one of those paper flowers the farmers carried in procession in his native province.

"Good! Good!" the president exclaimed. "You really do play extremely well. In fact, young man, considering your age, weight and status, you must be one of the most promising violinists in the country."

Triclinio was visibly overcome by emotion and almost oblivious to the flashing cameras of the journalists who had been dozing behind a screen.

"Nevertheless," the leader added, controlling his own emotion, "I did notice several mistakes."

As the president was speaking, Ufa shook her head in disagreement.

"Yes, my daughter, yes," the president went on. "It's a defect common to all violinists in this country. He is not the only one. The way you hold your bow shows that you have followed two different schools: the Franco-Belgian and the Russian, if I am not mistaken. Have you realized," he rounded on his aides, "why things are going so badly in this country? Anyway," he continued, turning to Ufa and Triclinio, "it's the best playing I have heard for a long time. Alas, it counts for nothing in this blessed land of fat cows."

The president suddenly got to his feet, lifted the violin, checked the tuning, and played some descending scales with double stopping, which revealed a precision worthy of some greater cause. Feeling uncomfortable in his cap, he removed it to reveal a head of lovely flaxen hair that resembled the blonde tints in Ufa's hair. Needing more freedom of movement for the broad strokes, he next unbuckled his sword and laid it on the table beside his cap. Then taking a deep breath, he launched into Tartini's sonata *The Devil's Trill*.

He played as if he had never done anything except play the violin: his right arm vigorous yet light as a butterfly, admirable suppleness in his left hand; relaxed to the full and intrinsically musical, as the critics would later report.

Triclinio, who could barely suppress an outburst of emotion, saw that Ufa was signalling her father to stop playing for a moment. When the president stopped, she approached him with filial devotion and removed the epaulette on his left shoulder to enable him to hold his instrument with greater ease. He acquiesced with his customary good nature and went on playing demo-cratically.

"The special fingering of the Italian maestro Sfilio?" Triclinio enquired of Ufa.

"Precisely. He studied semitones under the renowned Sevĉik but recently he started to adopt the conventions of the Italian school. It's tremendous."

"Why do you wear pigtails? They don't suit you at all." She blushed.

"I don't like them either, but I wear them here because of all the ambassadors who visit."

"I didn't mean to hurt your feelings."

"That's not why I blushed, you idiot. In a minute daddy will stop playing, the audience will be over, and now that you know who I am, you will no longer be interested in me. Are we ever likely to see you again?"

The president had finally stopped playing and was drying the perspiration on his forehead. He shook Triclinio by the hand and said in a gruff voice:

"I expect we'll meet again, my friend."

"I hope so. And many thanks for your advice."

The president then turned to the teleprinters and his aides who awaited him impatiently. Suddenly, he stopped in his tracks and saw Ufa and Triclinio holding hands. He told Triclinio:

"I am very sorry not to be able to do anything for you in the short term. To govern does not mean to hold power, and no one is safe here, not even me. If I remain in office for some time, you may be assured that I shall do something for you. It's demoralizing to cherish hopes that come to nothing."

The president walked away and one of his aides handed him an aspirin and a glass of water.

Triclinio suddenly remembered Palmira's trousseau and was gripped by the most terrible remorse. He hastily took his leave of Ufa and, avoiding the lift, went down the stairway taking the steps two at a time. For the first time in his life he was in a rush without really knowing where he was going, He wanted to bawl and shout like the drunkards of his native province, but then he reflected that the presidential palace was the presidential palace.

He was still racing downstairs in this frenzied state of mind when the lift door opened and Ufa stepped out.

Taking him by the poncho, she told him what we are
soon about to learn.

17

Triclinio shakes with fear

Ufa, fluttering like a flag at the top of a mast, clung to Triclinio and confessed that she was afraid.

"It's the same fear you experienced when they started firing tear-gas grenades in the theatre," Ufa went on. "Frankly, Triclinio, I'm terrified that something might happen to you. The noise you heard when the building shook was not an earth tremor or whatever you imagined. It was something very special. Don't you realize what is happening?"

"To be honest, no," Triclinio replied, overcome by fleeting happiness.

"How can you be unaware of what is happening? This affects all of us. How can you possibly not realize? It doesn't seem possible."

"My head becomes filled with sounds. I've had this illness since childhood, ever since my father talked to me about Paganini beside the river bank. And when I hear no sounds, I begin to despair for I, too, should like to know what is happening."

"Don't imagine that you're the only one who experiences this problem. This country is nothing but sound. Listen, Tricly, the situation is more serious than you think. We are being driven mad by sounds. Those who govern this country spend their lives singing. Now everybody is playing the guitar, but they play whatever comes into their head, without any conductor to guide them, and whenever anyone suggests hiring a conductor capable of putting things straight, everybody wants the job. They are more conceited than your arthritics."

"I think you should calm down a little."

"Calm down! Calm down! All this calm is getting on my nerves. But that is not what I wanted to talk about. As you were about to start playing the *Romanza*, the building began to shake, didn't it? My heart was in my mouth. And you behaved as if nothing was happening. Aren't you even aware of what took place?"

"I thought they were going to overthrow your father. He would not be the first president I've seen fall from power."

"I only wish they had! Believe me, since daddy became president there has never been a moment's peace in our house. Daddy used to be quite happy spending his days at home greasing his shotguns and listening to music by Rossini – he adores Rossini – despite mummy's obsession with cleanliness. Then one fine day, obeying the instincts of our wretched ancestors, he got the idea that he should conduct this orchestra *sui generis* which has cost us so many dollars and given us so many headaches. He's been taking pills ever since. I would give anything to see daddy smile again. Your visit today and your violin did cheer him up a bit. If only the building had not started to shake. That spoiled things. That's why he dismissed you so suddenly and why he played the *Trill*. Otherwise he would have played till dawn and then carried on playing at home, just as La Pacini used to come round to our house to sing arias that Marcelo had forbidden."

"I thought it was an earth tremor."

"That's what daddy's aides said. But it was not a

tremor. It was the torturers. Those same torturers who left your friends in Violinville arthritic. For while they never talk about it, their arthritis was not caused by humidity or lack of exercise. It was caused by the electric prod. It was the torturers down in the basement that made the building shake. Only the day before yesterday, they arrested a young chap like you and they are holding him, or at least they were holding him, in the cellars. They have cut out the stone of madness, by removing his brain. I can't tell you how terrifying it is."

"As for me," said Triclinio, trying to restrain the terrified beating of his heart, "my life has been full of adventures. But I have never known anything like this. This is the worst of all."

He lowered his head. He was ashamed of what was happening and felt guilty.

"What is worrying you?"

"I can't help feeling I'm to blame for all this."

"Good heavens! What are things coming to when the innocent start feeling guilty," Ufa exclaimed.

"I must do something about it. I still don't know exactly what, but I'm determined to stop these tortures."

"All right, but what are you going to do now? I'm more worried about the present situation than about any dangers ahead. Where are you going to go?"

"I'm still not sure," Triclinio replied, looking fierce. And letting go of Ufa's long blonde hair which he had been fondling, he tore himself away from her and swiftly left the audience chamber. Once outside the building, he suppressed a sudden impulse to trample the pigeons in the square, when he saw a presidential guard signalling to him to look up. There he saw Ufa on a balcony waving goodbye. He raised his arms and the pigeons took flight, filling the entire sky, as in an illustration of

Independence Day. Then Ufa, looking somewhat bashful, affectionately stuck out her pink, inviting tongue.

Triclinio disappeared down a sidestreet without realizing that the flying pigeons were not due to his presence but to a convoy of seventy tanks intent on war that were advancing menacingly on the presidential palace. He turned left then right, heading in the direction of the port, while the historic *March of San Lorenzo* could be heard on every radio blaring forth its stirring rhythms to the entire nation.

18

Hamelin

With the dollars which Ufa had slipped into his pocket, Triclinio bought suitable clothes to disguise himself as a blind man. Then he stationed himself on a strategic street corner near the Colon and started to play. At his feet a small placard read as follows: "Help me to finish my studies." In this way he found enough money to eat once a day and to rent a room for the night in a rundown hotel. He vowed he would never see Ufa or Palmira again until he had established some kind of truth.

Since he got bored playing all day long, he decided to play different musical genres. In the morning he played folk music, in the afternoon something romantic, and in the evening, the classics. His blind man's outfit was so successful that one of the arthritic violinists, who chanced to pass by, did not recognize him. He paused for a moment to listen, yawned as Triclinio played the Mendelssohn Concerto, and then threw a wire semiquaver into his tin, saying: "Forgive me, comrade, but that's all I've got."

One day, while Triclinio was playing the *Romanza* by Sarasate and hoping that a pair of shoes might stop in front of him, for that could mean a few coins, he recognized the click-clack of tapping heels coming along the pavement. It was Ufa. The tapping stopped, and there was a long silence as he went on playing the *Romanza*.

When he finished playing, the person standing in front of him stayed silent; he remained quiet as always, bearing the weight of all the compassion that extended from La Quiaca to Tierra del Fuego. Hearing a "ki ji, ki ji, ki ji", which was Ufa's latest manner of weeping, he maintained the impenetrable silence of a blind man from La Rioja in order to avoid feeling any remorse.

"Ki ji ki ji," the tearful voice of Ufa reached him more clearly. "The way you've behaved, it's obvious you no longer care about me."

Ufa opened her purse and tossed a Kennedy half-dollar into the powdered-milk tin in which he collected donations. Triclinio then heard the tapping of Ufa's heels as she walked over the cracked paving stones. He swallowed hard and patiently launched into a theme by Ginastera.

The *Caprice No. 24* by Paganini attracted the attention of a cripple. The rhythmic toc toc of his stick had already revived childhood memories for the blind youth. But what appeared to be a memory materialized into an imperious voice that Triclinio would have recognized anywhere.

"My son," the old man said in ringing tones, "don't you remember me? It's me, Spumarola, now almost your pupil, almost your grandchild."

"Maestro," Triclinio said.

"Don't call me maestro. I've never heard this caprice played with such perfection. All this, and you're living in such misery? Or have you money deposited in some bank which could help save me from spending my last days in Violinville?"

"As a matter of fact," said Triclinio, "I should have disguised myself as a deaf mute rather than as a blind man, for the one thing I don't want to do right now is to talk. Everything is words and nothing but words. What I need is a little peace and quiet."

"Things are going to change, they are undoubtedly going to change," the old man said, ceasing to tap. "We are reorganizing the Party, and believe me, we are undergoing some radical reforms. We have such a plan for the nation's future progress that things are bound to change when we assume power. Besides, we have an impressive number of new members."

"That's good," Triclinio said, checking the tuning as he prepared to resume playing.

"Chopin was most ungrateful to his great teacher Elsner, and I suppose this is a law of history. All I can say is that I gave you nothing, but I discovered all that is good in you. I do my begging on the next block, but my arthritis doesn't allow me to play the violin, so I've simply written on a placard: 'Please help a poor old grandad.' I stand there without budging, although I have neither children nor grandchildren, and I manage somehow."

This was what the old man was saying when a municipal roadsweeping machine passed, lifted him off his feet and carried him off down the street.

Fearing that Spumarola might be followed by a whole procession of living memories, Triclinio gathered up his belongings and stationed himself on the next corner of the Paseo Colon.

It appeared to be a bad spot because no one stopped. He tried out a number of brilliant compositions but despite the technical intricacy of the pieces, not a soul stopped to listen. He then decided to play some variations which he had composed on the theme of "I have a doll dressed in blue", and no sooner had he started playing than he heard some heavy footsteps come to a standstill.

The voice said to him:

"I'll give you whatever you ask as long as you stop playing that music. How much do you want to be silent?"

"An electric prod," Triclinio replied.

"I'll bring you one immediately, but do stop playing," he shouted.

The fellow departed on a screeching motorcycle with as much haste as his remorse allowed. Triclinio was convinced that he had hit lucky and went on playing the blue doll theme. A number of motorcycles and jeeps came to a halt, and their owners, in lugubrious voices, repeated what the first motorcyclist had said.

Triclinio stood up, scattered the tin of coins with a sharp kick and then set off playing his violin right in the middle of the road. He was heading east. From every corner of the city, wayward individuals emerged who followed slowly behind him, carrying electric prods, revolvers, high-intensity lamps, awls, corkscrews, and other instruments of torture. As Triclinio walked on, he found himself followed by more and more torturers, now crushed and defeated but still carrying their instruments in their hands. By the time Triclinio had walked some ten blocks, the procession of torturers extended as far as the eye could see. People watched from their balconies, just as at the time of the English invasions, to see what was happening. And what they saw was this procession of rats, as in the story of the Pied Piper of Hamelin, trailing behind a prodigious violinist. The torturers, weeping like penitents and trying to conceal their knives, swords and hatchets, were visible to everyone and forgotten by no one. Triclinio was exhausted, but the mothers gave him heart. As more and more torturers appeared, it became increasingly difficult for him to draw sounds from his violin. The women encouraged him to press on, for they were relying on him to rid them of this plague. And the children who were old enough to have experienced tear-gas or the electric prod waved him on with small flags and handkerchiefs.

When they reached the river, Triclinio, still playing his violin, climbed up a ship's mast, while the torturers threw their instruments of torture into the sea.

As dusk fell, the wretched creatures slowly disappeared into the night, terrified that Triclinio might detain them. However, he had stopped playing and was lost in deep meditation.

Soon everyone had vanished. The balcony windows were closed and the city asleep. A ship's siren sounded in the distance. Triclinio's wan smile was reflected in the water as he contemplated, from the top of the mast, the lights of the universe flickering across river and sea.

19

The rectification of the initial error
of the founders

A colourless air descended over Buenos Aires. The air was so clear that the birds floated instead of flying. Triclinio climbed down from the mast and walked through the sunlit streets. The women sang as they swept the pavements and marvelled at the freshness and warmth in the air. People greeted one another with effusive good-mornings, their smiles extending like parasols. The sun-spots had vanished forever and on all sides the entire city revealed its attractions like a beautiful woman for all to admire. In the public squares, frail little pensioners acclaimed Triclinio and gave heartfelt salutes with their walking sticks. The cool shadows of young girls in flower replaced those of the solitary ombu trees long since felled by legends.

The volume of the instruments of torture raised the water level and brought flooding to those parts of the city built on the river. However, the flood was mitigated by the floating corpses of the torturers which formed a great barrier reef on the embankments. Once deprived of their instruments of torture, they had become as blind and deaf as moles. And without any music to guide them, for Triclinio's violin was silent, they had plunged to the depths of the river and reached the caves inhabited by electric fishes. Immutable laws had converted the torturers into corpses which now made up a floor on which grass could be sown.

The transparency of the atmosphere had even affected Triclinio, who for different reasons found himself floating rather than walking through the streets. A beggar in Congress Square, who was sleeping at the foot of the monument, told him how his friend, the violin-playing president, had been overthrown. When the president realized that all was lost, he asked to be left alone. He dismissed the presidential guards, who would have been obliged to give up their lives for him. Shut away in the room adjacent to the audience chamber, he put the *Adagio* by Albinoni on the record player and awaited the arrival of the new president and the nerve gas. The old man explained that the concert had been transmitted to the entire nation by the state broadcasting network and that everyone had been struck by curious modifications to the original score; it was as if the orchestra accompanying the organ had been playing phrases from another work. In fact what had happened was that the president, upon removing his cap and holding his head of flaxen hair in his hands, had allowed a tear to trickle onto the record, thus producing this strange sound. The dissonance, the old man told him, was much applauded by the arthritics of Violinville, but the new government saw their approbation as a betrayal of the Fatherland and announced its intention of erasing Violinville from the map. However, thanks to the intervention of the Pope, the International Red Cross and various clubs and associations throughout the world, the arthritics were left to end their days there.

This news saddened Triclinio, all the more so when he learned that the new government intended to ban music of any kind, thereby declaring a new form of independence. Brooding over these matters, he arrived at Constitution

Square, and with the silver half-dollar tried to buy a ticket for La Rioja. The ticket clerk explained that they could sell him a ticket for Cordoba, Catamarca or San Juan, but not to La Rioja, because it had been divided up and handed over to the aforementioned provinces. The new government had solved the burdensome problem of La Rioja by eliminating the province. With the new political division, the Cordillera region was given to San Juan, the northern region to Catamarca and what was left to Cordoba. The inhabitants of Cordoba had installed a sausage factory in the governor's palace and the governor himself had been given a job as porter in the Law Courts of San Juan. The history of the province became material for humorous anecdotes and sambas, the archway at the entrance to the defunct city was converted into an oven for baking meat pies, the lumberjacks of the Llanos were castrated and their wives given artificial insemination with products imported from Japan. The provincial capital was screened off with stalls, the towns of the interior ploughed up, and a bishop who offered resistance was demoted to the rank of altar-boy at the suggestion of the Cardinal. Finally, the dogs, chickens, donkeys and street sellers were classified together under the heading of "miscellaneous", and were then packed and despatched to Bolivia in payment of some debt or other. A number of folk musicians escaped the levy and remained concealed for some time amidst the scrubland near the devastated villages, and people say that at night their pitiful songs can still be heard in the mountains. But those who wished to give them a new life never succeeded in tracking them down.

The ticket clerk at the bus station told Triclinio the whole story while showing him newspaper cuttings and maps with the new boundaries of the provinces which had annexed La Rioja. Triclinio read all the information available in the hope of discovering what had happened to the bees, but found nothing.

He then realized that he had no roots and that there was no force to carry him anywhere. Feeling rather weary of life, but with some strength left, he gazed over Buenos Aires.

The city suddenly lost the transparency observed in the morning, when it could be viewed at a glance. Everything was now as opaque as before. Triclinio could scarcely see the buildings on the opposite side of the pavement and the backs of the people walking in front of him. From the workshops and factories came the frenzied beating of hammers, the grating of metal, the furious hissing of saws that caused the metal to quiver as new instruments of torture were manufactured.

Triclinio still had his violin, which lay weightless in his idle, calloused hands, and a host of memories which reverberated like the saws and hammers in the workshops. He was hungry and felt a little cold. Huddling up in a doorway, he fell asleep.

In his dreams he heard a lorry driving slowly and stopping every couple of minutes. He heard footsteps as men ran to and fro collecting dustbins. He then felt himself being raised off the ground like Spumarola and dropped onto a heap of refuse amidst papers, banana skins, discarded corks and jars of beauty cream.

He awoke to find himself on a rubbish dump and he lay there gazing at his silver half-dollar. He covered his violin to prevent it from being damaged by wind and water. Later he wandered off aimlessly, heading nowhere and suddenly he spied a lagoon. It was the lagoon of Violinville.

20

A city for Triclinio

Before entering the town, he put the silver half-dollar inside the pass which Ufa had also given him and threw them into the water. He crossed the lagoon with difficulty and strode out towards the town. The six arthritics were waiting to greet him, and behind them were all the other inhabitants, playing instruments that resembled guitars and singing songs never heard on the radio: songs that reminded him of the ballads sung by humble peasants in the fields of his native province. Over the bridge, instead of a treble clef made of wire there was an arch made of the same material, just like the arch over the entrance to his former city. "This is La Rioja!" Triclinio exclaimed. Bees hovered around him in search of flowers and then flew off towards the Palermo gardens. The streets were crammed with beehives, kiosks selling magazines, donkeys and cactuses. Using cardboard boxes and sacking, the inhabitants had also made mountains that were ill-placed geographically, and with the instrument-cum-statue reconstructed the Governor's palace, as well as the social club, the cathedral, and the snack bar in Benjamin de la Vega Street.

The musicians stopped playing and, leading Triclinio by the hand, took him on a tour of the city. The social workers had darkened their faces with coal in order to resemble the girls from the interior of La Rioja, and they walked slowly as if intimidated by Triclinio's presence. A number of bootblacks offered to polish his shoes, but Triclinio declined, explaining that the shoes did not belong to him.

With pieces of broken mirrors gathered from the nearby rubbish dump, the arthritics had succeeded in making the pallid sun blaze through the streets of Violinville. The bleating of goats semi-entangled in the nearby mountain of sacking greeted Triclinio, who looked at everything without thinking of anything.

The houses of tin and cardboard closely resembled those of his native province. "A few days ago they resembled them even more, but now they have been fumigated twice and sprayed all over with coloured water," one of the arthritics informed Triclinio. A hefty lad rode past on a bicycle made almost entirely from scrap metal from the rubbish dump. As he rode, the cyclist was making the noise of a motorcycle without a silencer. This made Triclinio smile. Looking westwards, he saw a somewhat higher mountain, its summit sprinkled with flour: it was Famatina. "Obviously gold and silver mines cannot be produced at will. Everything you see there is just as you described it to us. If there is anything missing, that is because you forgot to mention it," they told him.

Triclinio paused before a house made from polythene bags and recognized it as being the house of an old friend. "Of course, and that is your house," one of the arthritics said, pointing ahead. Indeed, it was his house, or, at least, resembled his house, with a stream that had dried up, half-withered trees and an oven for baking bread. He stepped inside, trembling with fear and with that painful happiness which had gripped him the moment he entered the town.

At the back of the house, a little bearded old man who tended the beehives told him jokingly that a certain Spumarola had arrived from Buenos Aires and that it would be a good idea to study the violin with him. Then the old man gave Triclinio some dried figs for lunch and, indicating a real mattress, invited him to take an afternoon nap.

Triclinio stretched out with pleasure, ready for sleep, but there was far too much shouting from the stallholders on the street. He could make out from their cries that they were selling homemade bread, pancakes and meat pies, but he could not understand the vegetable sellers, whose cries were distorted by the loudspeakers.

The old man stretched out on another pallet which was in the same room and asked Triclinio if he was sleeping.

"How can I sleep with all these people shouting?"

"They are your people, are they not?"

"Yes, I know, and that's why I don't want to sleep."

The old man who was behaving like his father asked him to listen attentively to another kind of sound. Triclinio listened, and heard the noise of running water coming from the stream.

A moment later, Triclinio asked the old man if he was sleeping. He replied that he was not, he was simply passing the time. He then added: "And now I am going to tell you about the life of Paganini which I read in one of those magazines they send from Buenos Aires."

When they got to Paganini's love affairs, Triclinio asked:

"And Palmira?"

"What about Palmira?" the old man asked, searching for a reply to cover his ignorance. "She must be waiting for you somewhere."

"She was sewing her trousseau," Triclinio recalled.

The old man raised his head to tell him that it was a little premature to be thinking about these things.

"There are still a number of things to be settled, but no one will deny you love, for that is something to which we are all entitled. Everything must be cleared so that when love finally arrives it will be into a world prepared, just like those newborn babies who find that they already possess little bootees and baby clothes and all those other things they need in order to start life on this earth."

The old man went on counselling him for some time but Triclinio was falling asleep and no longer listened, just as he had stopped listening when his father spoke to him about Paganini, because not only did these things seem unimportant but his head was becoming filled with sounds. When the old man realized that Triclinio was no longer listening, he got up and gave him a shake to awaken him. He then said:

"I am the oldest person here, and I have survived more misfortunes than anyone. But thanks be to God, I don't suffer from arthritis and I could play a real violin as well as I play this imaginary one. But I have sworn that I shall never play a real violin again until we know what fate has in store for us."

Triclinio, without having grasped the meaning of these words, replied between dreams: "That's fine. That's fine. We can talk about it later. We have all the time in the world."

Reassured that Triclinio was still sleeping, the old man returned to his pallet and, lying on his back, he began to listen attentively to the *Concerto for Cats and*

Horns which the six arthritics were performing at this very moment beneath a tin-plated moon.

OTHER TITLES
·FROM·
SERPENT'S TAIL

NON FICTION

IAN BREAKWELL   *Ian Breakwell's Diary*
NOAM CHOMSKY   *The Chomsky Reader*
LANGSTON HUGHES   *The Big Sea*
CHARLES JOHNSON   *Being and Race*
CLAUDE MCKAY   *A Long Way From Home*
KLAUS MANN   *The Turning Point*
TOM WAKEFIELD   *Forties' Child*

M   A   S   K   S

NEIL BARTLETT   *Who Was That Man?*
MICHAEL BRACEWELL   *The Crypto-Amnesia Club*
IAN BREAKWELL   *The Artist's Dream*
LESLIE DICK   *Without Falling*
JANICE EIDUS   *Faithful Rebecca*
ALISON FELL (ed.)   *The Seven Deadly Sins*
JUAN GOYTISOLO   *Landscapes After the Battle*
JUAN GOYTISOLO   *Marks of Identity*
STEVE KATZ   *Florry of Washington Heights*
RAUL NUÑEZ   *The Lonely Hearts Club*
LUISA VALENZUELA   *The Lizard's Tail*

Juan Goytisolo
LANDSCAPES AFTER THE BATTLE

'Eloquent and profound . . . needs reading every-where.'
                                    THE INDEPENDENT

'Juan Goytisolo is one of the most rigorous and original contemporary writers . . . *Landscapes After the Battle* [is] an unsettling, apocalyptic work, splendidly translated by Helen Lane.'
                                    MARIO VARGAS LLOSA

'Fierce, highly unpleasant, and very funny.'
                                    THE GUARDIAN

176 pages £7.95 (paper)

MARKS OF IDENTITY

'For me *Marks of Identity* was my first novel. It was forbidden publication in Spain. For twelve years after that everything I wrote was forbidden in Spain. So I realized that my decision to attack the Spanish language through its culture was correct. But what was most important for me was that I no longer exercised censorship on myself, I was a free writer. This search for and conquest of freedom was the most important thing to me.'

Juan Goytisolo, in an interview with CITY LIMITS

304 pages £8.95 (paper)

Luisa Valenzuela
THE LIZARD'S TAIL

'Luisa Valenzuela has written a wonderfully free ingenious novel about sensuality and power and death, the "I" and literature. Only a Latin American could have written *The Lizard's Tail*, but there is nothing like it in contemporary Latin American literature.'   SUSAN SONTAG

'By knotting together the writer's and the subject's fates, Valenzuela creates an extraordinary novel whose thematic ferocity and baroque images explore a political situation too exotically appalling for reportage.'   THE OBSERVER

'Its exotic, erotic forces seduce with consummate, subliminal force.'   BLITZ

'Don't classify it as another wonder of "magic realism": read, learn and fear.'   TIME OUT

'*The Lizard's Tail* will probably sell far fewer copies than Isabel Allende's inferior *Of Love and Shadows*, and that is a great pity. [It] is a wild adventurous book . . . a gripping and challenging read.'
   THIRD WORLD QUARTERLY

288 pages £7.95 (paper)

Jorge Amado
DONA FLOR AND HER TWO HUSBANDS

Dona Flor's first husband, a notorious gambler and womanizer, has unexpectedly died. When the local pharmacist proposes to her, she accepts his hand in marriage. However, he is unable to satisfy her erotic visions. Then one night her first husband materializes at the foot of her bed . . .

'Jorge Amado has been writing immensely popular novels for fifty years. His books are on the grand scale, long, lavish, highly coloured, exuberant. . . . Amado has vigour, panache, raciness . . . a reputation as a master storyteller.'   TLS

'a bacchanalia of a book: a veritable orgy of sex, food, gambling and mayhem'   CITY LIMITS

576 pages £7.95 (paper)